HERZEGOVINA

# Herzegovina
George Arbuthn

# HERZEGOVINA

# HERZEGOVINA

## CHAPTER I.

Object of Travels--Start--Mad Woman--Italian Patriot--Zara--Sebenico--Falls of Kerka--Dalmatian Boatmen--French Policy and Austrian Prospects--Spalatro--Palace of Diocletian--Lissa--Naval Action--Gravosa--Ragusa--Dalmatian Hotel--Change of Plans.

'Omer Pacha will proceed with the army of Roumelia to quell the disturbance in Herzegovina.' Such, I believe, was the announcement which confirmed me in the idea of visiting the Slavonic provinces of European Turkey. Had any doubts existed in my mind of the importance attached by the Ottoman government to the pacification of these remote districts, the recall to favour of Omer Pacha, and the despatch of so large a force under his command, would have sufficed to remove them. As it was, the mere desire to keep myself au courant of the events of the day, together with the interest which all must feel in the condition of a country for whom England has sacrificed so much blood and treasure, had made me aware that some extraordinary manifestation of feeling must have occurred to arouse that apathetic power to so energetic a measure. Of the nature of this manifestation, little or no reliable information could be obtained; and so vague a knowledge prevails touching the condition of these provinces, that I at once perceived that personal observation alone could put me in possession of it. The opinions of such as did profess to have devoted any attention to the subject, were most conflicting. Whilst some pronounced the point at issue to be merely one between the Turkish government and a few rebellious brigands, others took a far more gloomy view of the matter, believing that the first shot fired would prove the signal for a general rising of the Christian subjects of the Porte, which, in its turn, was to lead to the destruction of Turkish suzerainty in Europe, and to the consummation of the great Panslavish scheme. To satisfy myself on these points, then, was the main object of my travels,--to impart to others the information which I thus obtained, is the intention of this volume.

On August 31, 1861, I left Trieste in the Austrian Lloyd's steamer, bound for Corfu, and touching en route at the ports on the Dalmatian coast. Having failed in all my endeavours to ascertain the exact whereabouts of the Turkish head-quarters, I had secured my passage to Ragusa, reckoning on obtaining the necessary information from the Ottoman Consul at that town; and in this I was not disappointed.

It is not my intention to enlarge upon this portion of my travels, which would indeed be of little interest; still less to tread in the steps of Sir Gardner Wilkinson, whose valuable work on Dalmatia has rendered such a course unnecessary; but rather to enter, with log-like simplicity, the dates of arrival and departure at the various ports, and such-like interesting details of sea life. If, however, my landsman-like propensities should evince themselves by a lurking inclination to 'hug the shore,' I apologise beforehand.

My fellow-passengers were in no way remarkable, but harmless enough, even including an unfortunate mad woman, whose mania it was to recount unceasingly the ill-treatment to which she had been exposed. At times, her indignation against her imaginary tormentors knew no bounds; at others, she would grow touchingly plaintive on the subject of her wrongs. That she was a nuisance, I am fain to confess; but the treatment she experienced at the hands of her Dalmatian countrymen was inconsiderate in the extreme. One who professed himself an advocate for sudden shocks, put his theory into practice by stealing quietly behind his patient, and cutting short her lugubrious perorations with a deluge of salt water. This was repeated several times, but no arguments would induce her to allow her wet clothes to be removed, so it would not be surprising if this gentleman had succeeded in 'stopping her tongue' beyond his expectations. The only other lady was young and rather pretty, but dismally sentimental. She doated on roses, was enamoured of camelias, and loved the moon and the stars, and in fact everything in this world or out of it. In vain I tried to persuade her that her cough betrayed pulmonary symptoms, and that night air in the Adriatic was injurious to the complexion.

The man-kind on board included an Austrian officer of engineers, a French Consul, and a Dalmatian professor. Besides the above, there was an Italian patriot, whose devotion to the 'Kingmaker' displayed itself in a somewhat eccentric fashion. With much mystery, he showed me a portrait of Garibaldi, secreted in a watchkey seal, while his waistcoat buttons and shirt studs contained heads of those generals who served in the campaign of the Two Sicilies. It was rather a novel kind of hero-worship, though, I fear, likely to be little appreciated by him who inspired the thought.

September 1.--Landed at Zara at 6.30 A.M., and passed a few hours in wandering over the town and ramparts. These last are by no means formidable, and convey very little idea of the importance which was attached to the city in the time of the Venetian Republic. The garrison is small, and, as is the case throughout Dalmatia, the soldiers are of Italian origin. The Duomo is worthy of a visit; while the antiquarian may find many objects of interest indicative of the several phases of Zarantine history. Here, in a partially obliterated inscription, he may trace mementos of Imperial Rome; there, the Campanile of Santa Maria tells of the dominion of Croatian kings; while the winged lion ever reminds him of the glory of the Great Republic, its triumphs, its losses, and its fall. On leaving we were loudly cheered by the inhabitants, who had collected in large numbers on the shore. A few hours' run brought us abreast of Fort St. Nicholas, and ten minutes later we dropped anchor in the harbour of Sebenico. Here the delight of the people at our arrival was somewhat overwhelming. It vented itself in an inordinate amount of hugging and kissing, to say nothing of the most promiscuous hand-shaking, for a share of which I myself came in. My first step was to negotiate with four natives to row me to the Falls of Kerka, about three hours distant. This I had succeeded in doing, when, having unfortunately let them know that I was English, they demanded seven florins in place of four, as had been originally agreed. Resolving not to give way to so gross an imposition, I was returning in quest of another boat, when I met a troop of some six or seven girls, young, more than averagely good-looking, and charmingly dressed in their national costume. I presume that my T.G. appearance must have amused them; for they fairly laughed,--not a simpering titter, but a good honest laugh. To them I stated my case, and received a proper amount of sympathy. One offered to row me herself, while another said something about 'twenty florins and a life,'--which, whatever it may have meant, brought a blush to the cheek of the pretty little volunteer. At this juncture the boatmen arrived, and on my assurance that I was perfectly satisfied with the company to which they had driven me, which my looks, I suppose, did not belie, they came to terms. Leaving the bay at its NW. extremity, where the Kerka flows into it, we proceeded about four miles up that river. At this point it opens out into the Lake of Scardona, which is of considerable size, and affords a good anchorage. There is an outlet for the river to the N., close to which is situated the little town of Scardona. The banks of the river here begin to lose their rocky and precipitous appearance, assuming a more marshy character, which renders it unhealthy in the summer. The Falls are approached by a long straight reach, at the end of which they form a kind of semicircle, the entire breadth being about 250 feet. In winter, or after heavy rains, the effect must be very grand; but at the time of my visit they were, in consequence of the great drought, unusually small. Below the falls is a mill worked by a Levantine, who appears to drive a flourishing trade, grinding corn for Sebenico, Zara, and many other places on the coast.

The Dalmatian boatmen are a very primitive set in everything save money matters. One asked, Are the English Christians? while another asserted most positively, that he had taken an Englishman to see the Falls in the year 1870. Their style of rowing resembles that in vogue among the Maltese and Italians, excepting that they make their passenger sit in the hows of the boat. This, at any rate, has the advantage of keeping him to windward of themselves, which is often very desirable. Another point of difference is, that they wear shoes or slippers,--the latter being, in some instances, really tasteful and pretty.

The moon was high ere we reached the ship, where I found all the passengers assembled upon deck. One after another they disappeared below, until I was left alone. I know no spot so conducive to reflection as the deserted deck of a ship at anchor on a lovely night, and in a genial latitude. In this instance, however, my thoughts assumed more of a speculative than retrospective character, large as was the field for the indulgence of the latter. The shades of emperors and doges faded away, giving place to the more terrestrial forms of living sovereigns; and the wild shouts of the Moslem conquerors resolved themselves into the 'Vive l'Empereur' of an army doing battle for an idea. Let Austria look to herself, that, when the hour of struggle shall arrive, as arrive it will, she be not found sleeping. Should Napoleon once more espouse the Italian cause, should he hurl his armies upon the Quadrilateral, who can doubt but that a diversion of a more or less important character will be attempted in the rear of the empire? But even though he should let slip the notable occasion presented to him by a rising among the Italian subjects of Austria, the evil day will only be postponed. I believe that, not content with the humiliation of that power at Villafranca, he will take advantage of any opportunity which disorder in the neighbouring Turkish provinces may offer him to aim a blow at her on her Dalmatian frontier, as a means to the gigantic end of crippling her, and with her ultimately the entire German Confederation. It is a great scheme, and doubtless one of many in that fertile brain. If Austria should resolve to defend her Venetian territory, as it may be presumed she will, she should spare no labour to strengthen her fortresses in the Adriatic. On the Dalmatian coast, Zara, Lissa, Pola, and Cattaro are all capable of making a very respectable defence in the event of their being attacked; while, to quote the words of Rear-Admiral Count Bernhard von Wüllersdorf and Urban, 'An Austrian squadron at Cattaro would be very dangerous to any hostile squadron on the Italian coast, as its cruisers would cut off all transports of coal, provisions, &c. &c.,--in a word, render the communication of the hostile squadron with the Mediterranean very difficult.... Lissa is the keystone of the Adriatic. This island, the importance of which in former times was never denied, commands the straits which lead from the southern to the northern half of the Adriatic.... The naval force at Lissa ought to be a local one, consisting of light fast gun-boats to cruise in the narrow waters, to which might be added some plated ships to keep open communications, on the one hand, between Lissa and the mainland, and on the other hand acting with the gun-boats to bar the passage to hostile vessels.' The publication of the article from which the above is extracted in the 'Oesterreichische Militar Zeitschrift,' proves sufficiently that the Austrian government is aware of the necessity which exists for taking precautionary measures; and the lesson which they learnt in 1859 ought to have induced them to adopt a more energetic policy in their military and naval affairs.

The defences of Sebenico consist of three small forts: St. Nicholas, containing seventeen mounted guns, is at the entrance of the bay, while San Giovanni and Santa Anna, situated on rising ground, command the town, harbour, and land approaches. The precise number of guns which they contain, I was unable to learn. The very meagre character of the information which I am in a position to impart on these subjects requires, I am aware, some apology. The difficulty of obtaining it during the short stay of a steamer must be my excuse. May it be accepted!

September 2.--Steamed into the port of Spalatro at 10.30 A.M. There is both an outer and inner harbour, the latter affording a good anchorage to vessels of any burden; yet, notwithstanding this, we were compelled, for the first time since leaving Trieste, to lie off at some distance from the quay. The origin of Spalatro dates from the building of the palace of Diocletian in 303, A.D. This glorious pile, however much it may offend against the rules of architecture, is well entitled to rank among the noblest monuments of imperial Rome. Its mammoth proportions, the novelty of conception evinced in many parts, together with its extraordinary state of preservation, render it alike unique, while the circumstances connected with its building impart to it an unusual interest. Wearied with the affairs of state,

Diocletian retired to Salona, where he passed the remaining nine years of his life in profound seclusion. Of the use to which he applied his wealth during that period, a record still exists in the golden gate and the Corinthian columns which decorate that regal abode; while we learn what were his pursuits from his own memorable reply to Maximian, when urged by him to reassume the purple. 'Utinam Salonis olera nostris manibus insita invisere posses, de resumando imperio non judicares;' or, as it has been somewhat freely translated by Gibbon-- 'If I could show you the cabbages I have planted with my own hands at Salona, you would no longer urge me to relinquish the enjoyment of happiness for the pursuit of power.'[A]

Nor has nature been less bountiful than man to this most favoured spot. The description given by Adams conveys a very accurate impression of the character of the surrounding country. 'The soil is dry and fertile, the air pure and wholesome, and, though extremely hot during the summer months, the country seldom feels those sultry and noxious winds to which the coasts of Istria and some parts of Italy are exposed. The views from the palace are no less beautiful than the soil and climate are inviting. Towards the W. lies the fertile shore that stretches along the Adriatic, in which a number of small islands are scattered in such a manner as to give this part of the sea the appearance of a great lake. On the N. side lies the bay, which led to the ancient city of Salona, and the country beyond it appearing in sight forms a proper contrast to that more extensive prospect of water, which the Adriatic presents both to the S. and the E. Towards the N. the view is terminated by high and irregular mountains situated at a proper distance, and in many places covered with villages, woods, and vineyards.'[B] Like most other relics of antiquity, the time-honoured walls of Spalatro have been witnesses of those varied emotions to which the human heart is subject. Thither Glycerius the prelate retired, when driven by Julius Nepos from the imperial throne. There, too, in a spirit of true Christian charity, he heaped coals of fire on the head of his enemy, by affording him a sanctuary when dethroned in his turn by Orestes, the father of Augustulus. Again, a little while, and within the same walls, where he had deemed himself secure, Julius Nepos fell a victim to the assassin's knife, and subsequently we find the houseless Salonites sheltering themselves within its subterraneous passages, when driven from their homes by the fury of the invading Avars. The memory of all these is passed away, but the stones still remain an undying testimony of a happy king.

Having passed some hours in the town and palace, I adjourned to one of the few small cafés in the principal street. While sipping my chocolate, I was accosted by an elderly priest, who most civilly enquired whether he could help me in any way during my stay at Spalatro. He proved to be a person of much intelligence, and, notwithstanding that his knowledge of English extended only to a few conversational words, he had read Sir Gardner Wilkinson's work on Dalmatia, and, as his remarks showed, not without profiting thereby. At 4.30 the same afternoon we arrived at Lissa, the military port of Austria in this part of the Adriatic. It is interesting to English travellers, its waters having been the scene of a naval action in which an English squadron, commanded by Captain Hoste, defeated a French squadron carrying nearly double as many guns. During the great war the island belonged to England, and indeed a portion of it is called to this day the Città Inglese. It at one time acquired a certain importance in a mercantile point of view, sardines being the staple article of commerce.

The same night we touched at Curzola, and at 4 A.M. on September 3 anchored at Gravosa, the port of debarcation for Ragusa. Taking leave of my friends on board, I landed at about 5 A.M., and, having committed my luggage, a small bullock trunk, saddle-bags, and a saddle, to the shoulders of a sturdy facchino, and myself to a very rickety and diminutive cart, I proceeded on my way to Ragusa. The drive, about a mile and a half in distance, abounds with pretty views, while the town of Ragusa itself is as picturesque in its interior detail as it is interesting from its early history. The grass-grown streets, the half-ruined palaces, and the far niente manners of the people, give little indication of the high position which the Republic once achieved. Yet, despite all these emblems of decay, there are no signs of abject poverty, but rather a spirit of frugal contentment is everywhere apparent.

Arriving at an hour when, in the more fastidious capitals of Europe, housemaids and milkmen hold undisputed sway, I found groups of the wealthier citizens collected under the trees which surround the café, making their morning meal, and discussing the local news the while. Later in the day ices and beer were in great demand, and in the evening the beauty and fashion of Ragusa congregated to hear the beautiful band of the regiment 'Marmola.' The hotel, if it deserve the name, is scarce fifty yards distant; it possesses a cuisine which contrasts favourably with the accommodation which the house affords.

The table d'hôte dinner is served in a kind of vaulted kitchen, the walls of which are hung round with scenes illustrative of the Italian campaign. The series, which comprises desperate cavalry charges, death wounds of general officers, and infantry advancing amidst perfect bouquets of shot and shell, closes appropriately with the pacific meeting of the two Emperors at Villafranca.

Here, then, I proposed to take up my quarters, making it the starting-point for expeditions to the Val d'Ombla, the beautiful Bocche di Cattaro, and Cettigne, the capital of Montenegro; but it was destined otherwise, and night found me on board a country fishing-boat, the bearer of despatches to Omer Pacha at Mostar, or wherever he might happen to be.

CHAPTER II.

Military Road to Metcovich--Country Boat--Stagno--Port of Klek--Disputed Frontier--Narentine Pirates--Valley of the Narenta--Trading Vessels--Turkish Frontier--Facilities for Trade granted by Austria--Narenta--Fort Opus--Hungarian Corporal--Metcovich--Irish Adventurer--Gabella--Pogitel--Dalmatian Engineer--Telegraphic Communication--Arrival at Mostar--Omer Pacha--Object of Campaign.

The change in my plans, and my precipitate departure from Ragusa, were the results of information which I there received. From M. Persich, the Ottoman Consul, whom I take this opportunity of thanking for his courtesy and kindness, I learned that the Turkish Generalissimo might be expected to leave Mostar for the frontier at any moment, and that the disturbed state of the country would render it perilous, if not impossible, to follow him thither. This determined me to push on at once, postponing my visit to Montenegro to a more fitting season. To make some necessary purchases, and to engage a servant, was the work of a few hours, and, being supplied by the Captano of the Circolo with the necessary visés and letters of recommendation to the subordinate officials through whose districts I should have to pass, it only remained to decide upon the mode of travelling which I should adopt, and to secure the requisite conveyance. My first point was Metcovich, a small town on the right bank of the Narenta, and close to the frontier lines of Dalmatia and Herzegovina. Three modes of performing the journey were reported practicable,--viz. on horseback, by water, or by carriage. The first of these I at once discarded, as both slow and tedious; the choice consequently lay between the remaining two methods: with regard to economy of time I decided upon the latter. But here a difficulty arose. The man who possessed a monopoly of carriages, for some reason best known to himself, demurred at my proceeding, declaring the road to be impassable. He farther brought a Turkish courier to back his statement, who at any rate deserved credit, on the tell-a-good-one-and-stick-to-it principle, for his hard swearing. I subsequently ascertained that it was untrue; and had I known a little more of the country, I should not have been so easily deterred, seeing that the road in question is by far the best which exists in

## HERZEGOVINA

that part of Europe. It was constructed by the French during their occupation of Dalmatia in the time of Napoleon, and has been since kept in good order by the Austrian government. Being thus thwarted in my plans, I made a virtue of necessity, engaged a country boat, and got under weigh on the evening of the day on which I had landed at Gravosa. The night was clear and starry; and as my boat glided along before a light breeze under the romantic cliffs of the Dalmatian coast, I ceased to regret the jolting which I should have experienced had I carried out my first intention. Running along the shore for some ten hours in a north-westerly direction, we reached Stagno, a town of small importance, situated at the neck of a tongue of land in the district of Slano, and which connects the promontory of Sabioncello with the mainland; ten minutes' walk across the isthmus brought us again to the sea. The luggage deposited in a boat of somewhat smaller dimensions, and better adapted for river navigation, we once more proceeded on our journey.

A little to the north of Stagno is the entrance to the port of Klek, a striking instance of right constituted by might. The port, which, from its entrance, belongs indisputably to Turkey, together with the land on the southern side, is closed by Austria, in violation of every principle of national law and justice.

Previous to 1852, many small vessels used to enter it for trading purposes, and it was not until Omer Pacha in that year attempted to establish it as an open port that Austria interfered, and stationed a war-steamer at its mouth.

In 1860 the restriction was so far removed that Turkish vessels have since been allowed to enter with provisions for the troops.

To the isolated condition of these provinces, coupled with the ignorance which prevails at Constantinople relative to the affairs of the interior, must be attributed the indifference which the Porte has as yet manifested regarding the preservation of its just rights. The importance to be attached to the possession by Turkey of an open port upon the coast cannot be overrated, since through it she would receive her imports direct from the producing countries, while her own products could be exported without being subjected to the rules and caprices of a foreign state. Nor are the Turkish officials in these quarters at all blind to the injury that accrues to Turkey, from the line of policy which Austria is now pursuing; but while they see and deplore the mildness with which their government permits its rights to be thus violated, they neglect to take any steps which might induce it to appeal to the arbitration of Europe. Were this done, there could be little doubt of the result; for, since the land on one side of the harbour, without question, belongs to Turkey, it would appear only just that she should have control over the half of the channel. But even were this to be accorded (which is most improbable, since it would prove dangerous to the trade of Trieste), the point at issue would still be far from settled. Any concessions will be unavailing so long as the present line of demarcation between the two countries shall exist; for while Turkey draws the line of limit from a point near the entrance of the harbour to the village of Dobrogna, Austria maintains the boundary to run from that village to a point farther within the port, by which arrangement she includes a small bluff or headland, which commands the entire harbour. She asserts her right to this frontier, upon the grounds of its having been the line drawn by the French during their occupation of Dalmatia. The Turks deny the truth of this, and state that the lines occupied by the French can still be traced from the remains of huts built for the protection of their sentries. Moreover, since the Austrians have also stated that the French, when in Dalmatia, did not respect the rights of the Sultan, but occupied Suttorina and Klek, the argument that they assume the frontier left them by the French is hardly entitled to much consideration. That Austria is very unlikely to open Klek of her own free will, I have already said; nor can she be blamed for the determination, since she must be well aware that, in the event of her doing so, English goods at a moderate price would find a far readier market than her own high-priced and indifferent manufactures. In a word, she would lose the monopoly of trade which she at present possesses in these provinces. But, on the other hand, were Turkey animated by a spirit of reprisal, she might throw such obstacles in the path of her more powerful neighbour as would almost compel her to abandon the system of ultra-protection.

The military road from Cattaro to Ragusa and Spalatro encroaches upon Turkish territory, and the telegraphic wire which connects Cattaro with Trieste passes over both Suttorina and Klek. The Austrian government would find it very inconvenient were the Porte to dispute the right of passage at these points. Should Turkey ever be in a position to force the adoption of the frontier, as defined by herself, the value of Klek in a military point of view will be immeasurably increased; for, while the port itself would be protected by her guns, the approach to it is perfectly secure, although flanked on either side by Austrian territory. The waters of the harbour open out into the bay of Sabioncello from seven to eight miles in width, so that a vessel in mid-channel might run the gauntlet with impunity.

Towards evening we entered the Narenta, the principal river of Dalmatia and Herzegovina, by one of the numerous mouths which combine to form its delta. Its ancient name was the 'Naro,' and it is also called by Constantine Porphyrogenitus 'Orontium.' Later it acquired an unenviable notoriety, as being the haunt of the

'Narentine Pirates,' who issued thence to make forays upon the coast, and plundered or levied tribute on the trading vessels of the Adriatic. At one time they became so powerful as to be able to carry on a regular system of warfare, and even gain victories over the Venetian Republic, and it was not till 997 A.D. that they were reduced to submission by the Doge Pietro Orseolo II., and compelled to desist from piracy.

The valley of the Narenta is but thinly populated, a circumstance easily accounted for by the noxious vapours which exhale from the alluvial and reed-covered banks of the stream.

The lowlands, moreover, which lie around the river's bed are subject to frequent and rapid inundations. Excepting one party of villagers, who appeared to be making merry around a large fire close to the bank, I saw no signs of human habitation.

The croaking of many frogs, and the whirr of the wild fowl, as they rose from their marshy bed at our approach, were the only signs of life to be perceived, though higher up we met a few rowing boats, and one of the small coasting vessels used for the transport of merchandise. These boats are generally from twenty to thirty tons burden, and are employed for the conveyance of ordinary goods from Trieste, whence the imports of Dalmatia, Bosnia, and the Herzegovina are for the most part derived. Their rates of freight are light, averaging from 10d. to 1s. per cwt., chargeable on the bulk. The more valuable or fragile articles are brought to Macarsca, a port on the Dalmatian coast, near the mouth of the Narenta, in steamers belonging to the Austrian Lloyd's Company, whence they are despatched by boat to Metcovich. The expense attendant on this route prevents its being universally adopted. Insurance can be effected as far as Metcovich at 1s. 4d. to 3s. 4d. per cwt. on the value declared, according to the season of the year.

Metcovich may be regarded as the Ultima Thulé of civilisation in this direction. Once across the frontier, and one may take leave of all one's preconceived ideas regarding prosperity or comfort. Everything appears at a standstill, whether it be river navigation or traffic on the land. The apathy of the Turkish government presents a striking contrast to the policy of Austria, who clearly sees the value to be attached to the trade of Bosnia and Herzegovina, and who, while throwing every obstacle in the way of competition, evinces unwonted energy to secure the monopoly which she now possesses. During the past few years she has granted many facilities for the growth of commercial relations between Herzegovina and her own provinces. Thus, for instance, the transit dues on the majority of imports and exports have been removed, a few articles only paying a nominal duty on passing into Turkey. Wool, skins, hides, wax, honey, fruits, and vegetables, are allowed into Dalmatia free of duty. A grant of 1,200,000 florins has, moreover, been recently made for the regulation of the channel of the Narenta, with the view of rendering it navigable by small steamers, which will doubtless prove a most profitable outlay. It is to be hoped that the Turkish government will take steps to continue the line to Mostar, which is quite practicable, and could be effected at a small expense.

The Narenta takes its rise at the foot of the small hill called Bolai, a spur of the Velesh range of mountains. Its route is very circuitous, the entire distance from the source to its mouth being about one hundred and thirty miles, while its average width is computed at about one hundred and forty yards. It is subject to rapid rises between the months of September and May, caused by rains in the mountains and the melting snow, and a rise of twelve feet in three or four hours is by no means uncommon. As a source of communication it might be invaluable to the province, but in its present state it is perfectly useless, since the hardness of its waters renders it unfit for irrigation. It has many tributary streams, amongst the most important of which are the Boona, Bregava, Rama, Radopolie, Trebitza, and Cruppa.

On its right bank, and some miles above the mouth, is a small town, which rejoices in the imposing name of Fort Opus, albeit it possesses neither walls, fortifications, nor other means of defence. As the night was already far advanced when we arrived, I resolved to stay there a few hours before continuing the row to Metcovich, which I should otherwise have reached before daylight, and have been compelled to lie off the town during the damp hours of morning. Neither sentry nor health officer appeared to interdict our landing; and having found a miserable outhouse, which served as a cabaret, I was preparing to snatch a few hours' sleep as best I might, when an Hungarian corporal, employed in the finance department, came to the rescue, and undertook to find me a bed. Of its quality I will abstain from speaking; but such as it was, it was freely given, and it took much persuasion to induce the honest fellow to accept any remuneration. His post can hardly be a pleasant one, for malaria and fever cause such mortality, that the station is regarded much in the same light as is the gold coast of Africa by our own government servants. As a set-off against these disadvantages, my friend was in receipt of 2d. per day additional pay. May he pass unscathed through the ordeal!

By 2 A.M. I had again started, and reached Metcovich at 5 A.M. on September 5. Here M. Grabrich, the principal merchant of the place, put me in the way of procuring horses to take me to Mostar, about nine hours distant. My destination becoming known, I was beset with applications for my good offices with Omer Pacha. Some of these were petitions for contracts for supplying the army, though the greater number were demands for arrears of payment due for the supply of meal, and the transport of horned cattle and other provisions to the frontier. One of the complainants, a Greek, had a grievance of a different and much more hopeless nature. He had cashed a bill for a small amount offered him by an Irish adventurer. This, as well as several others, proved to be forgeries, and the money was irretrievably lost. Although travelling under an assumed name, and with a false passport, I subsequently discovered the identity of the delinquent with an individual, whom doubtless many who were with Garibaldi during the campaign of the Two Sicilies will call to mind. He was then only remarkable for his Calabrian costume and excessive amount of swagger. When at Niksich I learned that he had escaped through that town into Montenegro, and he has not, I believe, since been traced.

No punishment can be too severe for a scoundrel who thus brings English credit into disrepute, and disgraces a name which, although little known in these regions, is deservedly respected.

From Metcovich the traveller may proceed to Mostar by either bank of the river. I was recommended to take the road on the northern side, which I did, and ten minutes' ride brought us to the frontier, where a custom-house official insisted upon unloading the baggage so recently arranged. In vain I remonstrated, and brandished my despatches with their enormous red seals in his face. His curiosity was not to be so easily overcome. When he had at length satisfied himself, he permitted us to depart with a blessing, which I acknowledge was far from reciprocated. The first place of any importance which we passed is Gabella. It stands on an eminence overhanging a bend of the river, by whose waters three of its sides are washed. In former days it was defended by two forts, whose guns swept the river in either direction, and commanded the approach upon the opposite bank. In A.D. 1694 it was taken by Cornaro, and remained in the hands of the Venetians until A.D. 1716, when they evacuated it, blowing up the greater part of its defences.

Immediately above the town, the Narenta traverses the plain of Gabella, which is one of the largest and most productive in the country.

The plains of Herzegovina are in reality nothing more than valleys or basins, some of which are so hemmed in by hills, that the streams flowing through them can only escape by percolation, or through subterranean channels. This last phenomenon frequently occurs, and no better example can be given of it than the

Trebinitza, which loses itself in the ground two or three times. After the last of these disappearances nothing is known for certain of its course, although a large river which springs from the rocks in the Val d'Ombla, and empties itself into the Adriatic near Ragusa, is conjectured to be the same.

Gabella, as well as Popovo, Blato, and other plains, is inundated in the winter, and remains in that state during three or four months.

They are traversed by means of punts, and excellent wild-duck shooting may be had by those who do not fear the exposure inseparable from that sport.

From this point the river entirely changes its aspect, losing the sluggish character which distinguishes it during its passage through the Austrian territory. Indeed, throughout its whole course, from its rise until it opens out into the plain of Gabella, its bed is rocky, and the current rapid and even dangerous, from the number of boulders which rise above the surface, or lie hid a little below the water line. It here receives the waters of the Trebisat or Trebitza, and the Bregava, the former flowing from the NW., the latter from the district of Stolatz in the SE. A few miles higher up is a narrow valley formed by two ranges of hills, whose rocky declivities slope down to, or in some places overhang, the river's bed. From one spot where the hills project, there is a pretty view of the town of Pogitel on the left bank. A large mosque, with a dome and minaret and a clock-tower, are the principal objects which catch the eye; but, being pressed for time, I was unable to cross the river, and cannot therefore from my own observation enter into any accurate details. The position is, however, exactly described by Sir Gardner Wilkinson as follows: 'It stands in a semicircular recess, like an immense shell, in the side of the hill, and at the two projecting extremities the walls run down from the summit to the river, the upper part being enclosed by a semicircular wall, terminated at each end by a tower.'

Half way between Metcovich and Mostar is a little village, which boasts an humble species of Khan.

Here I found the engineer in charge of the telegraph, a Dalmatian by birth. His head-quarters are at Bosna Serai, but he was then making a tour for the purposes of inspection and repair.

The telegraphic communication throughout the Ottoman Empire is now more general than its internal condition would warrant us in supposing. Indeed, in travelling through the country, one cannot fail to be struck by the strange reversal of the general order of things. Thus, for instance, both telegraph and railways have preceded the construction of ordinary roads.

And therein lies one of the principal causes of the hopelessness of Turkish civilisation; that it has been prematurely forced upon her, and that, in order to keep a position among the European nations, she is driven to adopt the highest triumphs of European intelligence without passing through the intermediate stages by which they have been acquired. The rapidly remunerative nature of a telegraphic service is obviously sufficient reason for its being thus early established; but its duties devolve entirely, not upon Turks, but upon the foreign employés of the government. It is, moreover, little used by the Mussulman population, and consequently tends but little to the enlightenment of the masses. On the subject of roads, I shall have occasion to speak hereafter, and must therefore beg the indulgent reader to accompany me along the bridle-path which takes us to the capital of Herzegovina.

Descending from the hills our progress became more rapid; yet, despite this, it was some hours after sunset before we entered the suburbs. As usual in a Turkish town, dogs and gravestones were to be found in abundance, the latter with their turbanned heads looking spectral and grim in the cold moonlight. Saving an occasional group of Mussulmans sitting silent and pompous in the dusty road, the city appeared perfectly deserted; and, as my now jaded ponies scrambled over the ill-paved streets, I began to speculate on the probability of passing the night al fresco. As may be conceived, then, it was with considerable satisfaction that I found myself, chibouque in hand, awaiting the arrival of the Pacha, who, notwithstanding the lateness of the hour, had expressed his intention of seeing me immediately. No one can have a greater horror than myself of that mania which possesses some travellers for detailing conversations with Eastern dignitaries, which, for the most part, consist of ordinary civilities, imperfectly translated by an half-educated dragoman.

In the present instance, however, I deem no apology necessary for dwelling upon this first or subsequent conversations; since anything from the lips of such a man at so critical a moment must, to say the least, be of interest, even though it should be without any actual political importance. Having discussed the relative attitudes of the European powers with regard to Turkey, and spoken most unreservedly on the subject of French and Russian intrigues, he expressed great interest in the opinions formed by the public of the different countries on the Herzegovinian and Montenegrin question. The principal topic of conversation, however, was the campaign then about to be opened against the Herzegovinian rebels, and the preparations which he had made for carrying it out.

While fully alive to the difficulties attending his task, resulting from political complications, and the physical features of the country, he ever spoke with confidence of the ultimate success of the Turkish armies and the general pacification of the country. If any man be competent to bring about this desirable consummation it is himself; for he possesses, to an eminent degree, that caution which is indispensable to the successful conduct of an offensive war in a mountainous country, and which is so much at variance with the haphazard arrangements usually found among Turkish generals.

In using the words offensive war, I mean to imply operations carried on from a regular base, and in accordance with the generally accepted rules of warfare, in contra-distinction to the guerilla fighting as practised by the insurgent mountaineers. In its more literal sense, Omer Pacha's mission can hardly be deemed offensive; his object is, not to overrun territory, nor even to seek a combat with the enemy, but rather to place the country in such a state of defence as will render it secure from the incursions of those brigands who, having thrown off the Turkish rule, have sought a refuge in the fastnesses of Montenegro, whence, in conjunction with the lawless bands of that province, they make forays across the frontier.


CHAPTER III.

Herzegovina--Boundaries--Extent--Physical Features--Mountains--Mineral Products--Story of Hadji Ali Pacha--Forests--Austrian Timber Company--Saw-Mill--Rivers--Towns--Villages--Population--Greek Catholics--Church Dignitaries--Roman Catholics--Monks--Franciscan College--Moral Depravity--Fine Field for Missionary Labour.

Herzegovina[C] or Bosnia Inferior, formerly the duchy of Santo Saba, is bounded on the N. by Bosnia, on the E. by Servia, on the W. by Dalmatia, and on the S. by Montenegro and the Adriatic.

Its greatest length, from Duvno in the NW., to Priepolie in the S., is about a hundred and twenty miles, and its greatest breadth from Konitza, on the Bosnian frontier, to the port of Klek, is about seventy-two miles.[D] It contains an approximate area of 8,400 square miles, with a population, of about thirty-five souls to the square mile.[D] A glance at any map, imperfect in detail as those yet published have been, will convey a tolerable idea of the nature of the country.

The ranges of mountains which intersect the greater part of the province are a portion of the Dinaric Alps. Along the Dalmatian and Montenegrin frontiers these are barren and intensely wild, and in many places, from the deep fissures and honeycomb formation of the rocks, impassable to aught save the chamois, the goat, or the indigenous mountaineer.

Proceeding inland, the country assumes a more habitable aspect: plains and pasture-lands capable of high cultivation are found at intervals, while even the mountains assume a more fertile appearance, and have a better depth of soil, which is well adapted for the cultivation of the olive and the vine. Dense forests, too, of average growth cover the mountain sides as we approach the Bosnian frontier, which, although inferior to those of Bosnia itself, would prove most remunerative to the government were they properly worked. But, unfortunately, the principle of isolation which the Porte has adopted with regard to these remote provinces, together with the want of enterprise among its inhabitants, the result of four hundred years of indolence on the one hand and oppression on the other, renders it problematical whether their ample resources will ever be developed. Should Turkey, however, arise from her lethargy, should genuine civilisation spread its branches over the land, we may then confidently anticipate a glorious future for her south-Slavonic provinces, doubting not that they will some day become 'the noblest jewel in their monarch's diadem.'

To convey an accurate idea of a province so little known as the Herzegovina, it will be best to enumerate the various physical features by which it is distinguished. Thus the highest and most important mountains are Dormitor in the district of Drobniak, on the Montenegrin frontier, and Velesh, which forms a rugged background to the plain of Mostar, the highest point being 6,000 feet above the level of the sea. Besides these, there are many others of nearly equal altitude, viz. Flam, Hergud, Prievolie, Vrau, Hako, Fartar, Belen, Stermoshnik, Bielevoda, Chabolie, Vrabcha, and Zavola. The perfect sea of rock which the southern part of the province presents to the eye is of grey limestone, varied however by a slatey stratum. Of the mineral products of the mountains little accurate knowledge prevails; gold, silver, and lead are said to exist, but I could not hear of their having ever been found to any extent. A firman was granted some years ago to one Hadji Ali Pacha, ceding to him for fifteen years the privilege of exploring Bosnia and Herzegovina, and working any mines which he might there discover. His application for this firman does not, however, in any way prove the existence of these minerals throughout the country generally, since it has proved to have been a mere cloak for diverting suspicion from many previous dishonest actions of which he had been guilty. His story is worthy of narration, as being no bad instance of the career of a Turkish parvenu, whose only qualifications were a little education and a large amount of effrontery.

Hadji Ali Pacha commenced his career as a clerk in the pay of the great Mehemet Ali Pacha, Viceroy of Egypt, but, having deserted to the Turks, he was employed by them in the capacity of Uzbashee or Captain. Fearful of falling into the hands of the Egyptians, he fled from his post, and, having made his way to

Constantinople, contrived, by scheming and bribery, not only to efface the memory of the past, but to secure the appointment of Kaimakan or Lieut.-Colonel, with which grade he was sent to Travnik in command of a regiment. Tahir Pacha, the Governor of Bosnia, had about this time been informed of the existence of some gold mines near Travnik, and ordered Hadji Ali to obtain samples for transmission to the Porte. This he did, taking care to retain all the valuable specimens, and forwarding those of inferior quality, which, on their arrival at Constantinople, were declared worthless. No sooner was this decision arrived at, than Hadji Ali imported the necessary machinery and an Austrian mechanic, to separate the gold from the ores, and in this way amassed immense wealth. Rumours having got abroad of what was going on, and the suspicions of Tahir being aroused, the unfortunate Austrian was put secretly out of the way, and, as a blind, the unprincipled ruffian procured the firman to which allusion has been made. It need hardly be said that he never availed himself of the privileges which it conferred upon him. Some time after these transactions, he applied for leave to visit Austria, on the plea of ill-health, but doubtless with the view of changing the gold. This was refused, and he was obliged to employ a Jew, who carried it to Vienna, and disposed of it there. In 1850, when Omer Pacha came to restore order in Bosnia, which had then revolted, Hadji Ali was sent with two battalions to the relief of another detachment; upon this occasion he communicated with the enemy, who cut off his rear-guard, and otherwise roughly handled the Turkish troops. Upon this, Omer Pacha put him in chains, and would have shot him, as he richly deserved, had he not known that his enemies at Constantinople would not fail to distort the true features of the case. He therefore sent him to Constantinople, where he was shortly afterwards released, and employed his gold to such good purpose, that he was actually sent down as Civil Governor to Travnik, which he had so recently left a prisoner convicted of robbery and treason. He was, however, soon dismissed for misconduct, and entered once more into private speculations. In 1857 he purchased the tithes of Bosnia and Herzegovina, and employed such ruffians to collect them as to make perfect martyrs of the people, some of whom were even killed by his agents. Exasperated beyond endurance, the people of Possavina rose en masse, and although the movement was put down without difficulty, it doubtless paved the way for the discord and rebellion which has been attended with such calamitous results. This is precisely one of those cases which has brought such odium on the Turkish government, and which may so easily be avoided for the future, always providing that the Porte be sincere in its oft-repeated protestations of a desire for genuine reform. Ali Pacha was at Mostar in the beginning of 1858, when the movement began, but was afraid to venture into the revolted districts to collect his tithes. The Governor, therefore, made him Commandant of the Herzegovinian irregulars, in which post he vindicated the character which he had obtained for cruelty and despotism. Subsequently he was appointed Kaimakan of Trebigné, but the European Consuls interfered, and he has now decamped, owing a large sum to government, the remnant of his contract for the tithes.

The sides of some of the mountains are covered, as I have before said, with dense forests of great value. There the oak, ash, elm, beech, walnut, red and white pine, and the red and yellow maple, grow in rich profusion, awaiting only the hand of man to shape them into 'the tall mast' and the 'stately ship.' But man, in these benighted lands, is blind to the sources of wealth with which his country teems, and to nature it is left in the lapse of years to 'consume the offspring she has herself produced.' The difficulty of transporting the timber to a market has been always alleged by the natives as their reason for neglecting to turn the forests to account; but this is a paltry excuse, for with abundance of rivers to float it to the coast, and a neighbour so anxious to monopolise the trade of the country as Austria has shown herself, little doubt can be entertained of the possibility of its advantageous disposal. As far back as 1849 an Austrian Company, foreseeing the benefits which would accrue from the employment of capital in these parts, obtained a concession of the pine forests for twenty years. Saw-mills were built near Mostar, and roads and shoots were constructed. About 5,000 logs had been cut and exported, when the works were stopped by Omer Pacha on his arrival to suppress rebellion in the country in 1850. This arbitrary measure on his part has been much reprehended, and does without doubt require explanation.

It should, however, be remembered that the contract, which was likely to prove most remunerative to the Company, and of but little advantage to the Turkish government, had been granted by Ali Pacha of Stolatz, the last Civil Governor, to

## HERZEGOVINA

whom a tithe of the products was being paid. He had in the meanwhile thrown off his allegiance, and consequently the only blame which can attach to Omer Pacha is a want of judgement, caused by over-zeal for the interests of his government. The case was afterwards litigated, and the Porte was mulcted 200,000 florins as an indemnity for their breach of the contract. This was liquidated from Ali Pacha's property, and the firman has been renewed for fourteen years since 1859. The Austrian government has, however, forbidden the Company to avail themselves of it, as its members are engaged in legal proceedings. The only saw-mill which I met with in the country was one at Boona, worked by an Hungarian, who is apparently doing a lucrative business.

The rivers in the country are of no great size or importance, but might in most cases be turned to account for the transport of timber or for irrigation. The waters of some of the large rivers, it is true, are injurious to vegetation from their hardness, but this does not apply to all. After the Narenta, the following are the most important:--the Trebenitza, Pria, Taro and Moratcha, Yanitza, Boona, Boonitza, Bregava, Kruppa, Trebisat or Trebitza, Drechnitza, Grabovitza, Biela, Kaladjin-Polok, and the Drina. It might be expected from its vicinity to Bulgaria, where such fine lakes are found, that the same would be the case in Herzegovina; but it is not so: Blato, which is marked as a lake in all maps, is only such in winter, as with early spring the waters disappear.

The only towns in the province worthy of mention, besides Mostar, are Fochia and Taschlijeh. They each contain about 10,000 inhabitants. The other towns are nothing more than large villages, with a bazaar. They are the seats of the district governments, such as Stolatz, Trebigné, Konitza, Niksich, Duvno, Chainitza, and others. The houses in these are not conspicuous for cleanliness, while those in the smaller villages are still less desirable as residences. They generally consist of some scores of huts, built of rough stones, without windows or chimneys, and roofed with boards, which are again covered with straw. They seldom contain more than one room, which the family occupies, in conjunction with the poultry and domestic animals. The furniture of these luxurious abodes consists of a hand-loom, two or three iron pots, a few earthen vessels, and some wooden spoons. The bedding is a coarse woollen blanket, which serves as a cloak in rainy or wet weather, and as a mattress and coverlet for the whole family, without distinction of sex.

The population of the Herzegovina amounts to about 182,000, divided as follows:--Catholics 52,000 Greek Church 70,000 Mussulmans 60,000

## HERZEGOVINA

Originally these were all of the same stock; and their present divisions, while constituting an element of safety for Turkey, are most prejudicial to the well-being of the country. The Greek faith predominates in the southern and eastern parts of the province. Its adherents are distinguished for their activity and cunning,--qualities which have rendered them far wealthier than their brethren of the Catholic communion. The possession of comparative wealth, and the consciousness of the moral support granted them by Russia, has made them presumptuous and over-bearing, hating alike all sects and creeds which differ from their own. Their ignorance is only equalled by the fanaticism which often results therefrom; and so bitter is their detestation of the Roman Catholics, that more than one instance has been known of its leading to foul acts of murder. Unoffending peasants have been taken in the revolted districts, and ordered to kneel and make the sign of the cross, to prove the truth of their assertions that they were not Mussulmans. The wretched creatures confidently did so in accordance with the Roman Catholic form, and their lives were unceremoniously forfeited to the bigotry and ferocity of their unrelenting judges. Nor are either tolerance or humanity in any way advocated by the priests, who are generally as illiterate and narrow-minded as their flocks, and whose influence, which is very great, is generally employed for evil. The priesthood are divided into Archimandrite, Igumens (chiefs of monasteries), Monks, and Priests, all of whom are natives of the province, where their whole lives have been passed. Of late years, however, many have been sent to receive their education in Russia. Some of these have now returned, but have not given signs of any desire to ameliorate the spiritual condition of the people. The Church has always been governed by a Vladika or Metropolitan, named from Constantinople. Like most other appointments from that capital, this was generally paid for, and its possessor consequently did not hesitate to employ every means in his power to reimburse himself. This, and the fact that he was never a native of the country, rendered him most unpopular; so that while the priests (little as they may deserve it) are regarded with reverence by the people, the Vladika was respected by neither the one nor the other. At present the office is vacant, none having been appointed since the demise of the last who occupied the episcopal chair. That event occurred in the commencement of 1861, and his attempts at extortion were so frequent and undisguised, that his death must have been felt as a great relief by the people. Petitions were sent at that time to Constantinople, praying for the appointment of a Slavish Metropolitan; but, independently of the difficulty of finding anyone of sufficient education among the Bosnian clergy, political considerations have induced the Porte to prevent the Patriarch complying with the demand; for, however bad in other respects they may have been, the

## HERZEGOVINA

Metropolitans have always remembered that their allegiance was due to the Patriarch of Constantinople, and not to the schismatic branch of the Greek Church, over which the Czar exercises both temporal and spiritual sway. Were a Slavish Metropolitan appointed, Russian influence would be dangerously augmented, and the task of transferring the allegiance of the people from their proper ecclesiastical head to the Russian Emperor, as has been attempted in Bulgaria, would here become easy of accomplishment.

In the N. and W. the Romish faith finds the greatest number of supporters, who look to Austria as their guiding star in all matters connected with religion. In their ranks are comprised the agriculturalists and artisans of the province, few being engaged in commerce. As regards education or enlightenment they are no farther advanced than their Greek compatriots: few can read or write their own language, and the knowledge of any other tongue is most exceptional. Learning, in its broader sense, is indeed confined exclusively to the convents, and, until very recently, no attempt of any kind was made by the priests to promote a desire for education or advancement among the people, their whole thoughts being bent on self-aggrandisement, and the acquisition of personal wealth. Careful enquiry has established the fact that no less than 60,000l. is annually paid in fees, penances, and gifts to the Church by the Roman Catholic section of the population; and we may fairly infer that the Greek priests extort an equally large sum. Of late schools have been established in different parts of the province, but the subjects of education are too confined to work any salutary change in the rising generation. Nor is it probably intended that such should be the case.

The Roman Catholics cordially return the hatred of the Greeks, marriages with whom are forbidden by the Catholic clergy. They are also inimical to the Mussulman population, by whom they are regarded as serfs. But this hostility is nurtured in secret, rarely displaying itself in overt acts of aggression. Four hundred years of oppression have completely broken their spirit, and they only ask to be allowed to enjoy in peace a fair portion of the fruits of their labour.

The Church is governed by two bishops. One, resident at Mostar, bears the title of Bishop of Azotto, and Vicar-Apostolic of the Herzegovina. The other, called the Bishop of Trebigné, lives at Ragusa, which is also included in his see. He has, however, a Vicar resident in the district of Stolatz. As in Bosnia, the monks are all of the Franciscan order. Considerable attention is paid to their education, and they are in every way immeasurably superior to the parochial clergy. In connection with that brotherhood a college has been for some years established, about twelve miles distant from Mostar. The subjects of education there are Latin,

Italian, Slavish, Church History, and Theology. From this college the students proceed to Rome, where they are admitted into the Franciscan order.

In the above remarks, I have endeavoured to show that the Christianity which exists in these provinces is merely nominal, since it is devoid of all those gentle and humanising principles which should distinguish it from Islamism, whose tenets have been ever propagated by conquest and the sword. The vices which more especially accompany and mar the beauty of true Christian civilisation here hold unrestrained dominion, and both Greeks and Catholics present a painful combination of western cunning and intrigue and oriental apathy, while they are devoid of that spirit of devotion and dignified resignation to the will of Providence which preeminently characterise the religion of Mahomet. Living on the confines of the two hemispheres, they have inherited the sins of each, without the virtues of either the one or the other. Nearly all adults are addicted to drunkenness, while the use of foul and indelicate language is almost universal,--men, women, and children employing it in common conversation. So long as such a state of things shall prevail, it is clearly impossible that any material improvement can be brought about; and until the people show some inclination to improve their own condition, the sympathy or consideration of others is uncalled-for and misplaced. The perpetual Russian whine about eight millions of Christians being held in galling subjection by four millions of Turks is a miserable deception, which, although it may serve as a pretext for their own repeated acts of interference, cannot mislead those who have seen anything of these countries, or who have been brought into contact with their Christian inhabitants. The most effective course, probably, which either the bitterest enemy or the warmest friend of the Ottoman government could pursue, would be to disseminate the seeds of true Christianity throughout the length and breadth of the land. And I say this advisedly; for on the future conduct of the Porte would depend whether such a course might lead to the establishment of Turkish supremacy, or to its irretrievable overthrow. That an enlightened nation, 'at unity in itself,' could cast off the yoke of an oppressive and tottering despotism can easily be imagined, while, on the other hand, a throne based upon principles of justice and progression would acquire fresh stability with each step made by its subjects in the path of civilisation. It is, indeed, strange that so fine a field for British missionary labour has been so long uncared-for and untried. Nowhere is there more ample scope for exertion of this nature than in the European provinces of Turkey; for while the Christian population could not but contrast the simple purity of the missionary life with the vicious habits and grasping avarice of their own clergy, the Mussulmans would see Christianity in a very different light from that in which they have been accustomed to regard it. Nor would any obstacles be thrown in the way by the Turkish government; nay, instances have even occurred of Protestant missionaries receiving encouragement and support: for, whatever may be said to the contrary, no nation is more tolerant of the exercise of other religions than these same much-abused Moslems. Whatever is to be done, however, should be done at once, for never was it more urgently needed. The American struggle seems to have paralysed the missionary labours of that nation, which had heretofore displayed much energy in proclaiming the glad tidings of great joy in these benighted lands. For England, then, it would appear, is reserved the noble task of rescuing these unfortunates from a state of moral darkness, as profound as that which envelopes the savage tribes of central Africa, or the remotest islands of the Pacific. That we have remained so long indifferent to the urgent appeals of the talented and earnest, though somewhat prejudiced, advocate of Slavonic institutions, Count Valerian Krasinski, is a matter of surprise and deep regret; for surely no country can be more replete with interest to Protestant England than that which may be regarded as the cradle of Protestantism, and whose fastnesses afforded a refuge during four centuries of persecution to the 'early reformers of the Church, the men who supplied that link in the chain which connected the simplicity of primitive doctrines with the present time.'

The affinity which exists between the Church of England in the early days of the Reformation and the Pragmatic section which glory in Huss and Jerome, is too close to be easily overlooked. Nor need Bosnia (taken collectively) succumb in interest to any Slavonic province, whether it be regarded as the stronghold of freedom of religious opinion, or as the scene of one of the greatest and most important triumphs of Islamism.

CHAPTER IV.

Introduction of Christianity--Origin of Slavonic Element--First Appearance of the Patarenes in Bosnia--Their Origin--Tenets--Elect a Primate--Disappearance--Dookhoboitzi, or Combatants in Spirit--Turkish Conquest--Bosnian Apostasy--Religious Fanaticism--Euchlemeh--Commission under Kiamil Pacha--Servian Emissaries--National Customs--Adopted Brotherhood--Mahommedan Women--Elopements--Early Marriages.

Authorities differ as to the time when Christianity was first introduced into Bosnia. Some say that it was preached by the apostle St. James, while others affirm that it was unknown until the year 853 A.D., when St. Cyril and Methodius translated the Scriptures into the Slavonic tongue; others again say that it dates back as far as the seventh century, when the Emperor Heraclius called the Slavonic nations of the Chorvats or Croats, and the Serbs or Servians, from their settlement on the N. of the Carpathian Mountains, to the fertile regions S. of the Danube. The warlike summons was gladly obeyed by those valiant men, who had unflinchingly maintained their independence, whilst their Slavish brethren, inhabiting the country between the Volga and the Don, had submitted to the iron yoke of the all-conquering Avars. These last were in their time expelled by the Croats and Serbs, and thus was Slavism established from the Danube to the Mediterranean. But these important results were not achieved without great sacrifice; and, wearied of war and bloodshed, the successful Slavonians devoted themselves to agriculture and industry, neglecting those pursuits which had procured for them a permanent footing in the Greek empire. Taking advantage of this defenceless state, resulting from their pacific disposition, Constans II. made war upon the country of Slavonia, in order to open a communication between the capital on the one side, and Philippi and Thessalonica on the other. Justinian II. (685-95 and 708-10) also made a successful expedition against the Slavonians, and transplanted a great number of prisoners, whom he took into Asia Minor. The Greek empire having become reinvigorated for some time under the Slavonian dynasty, Constantine Copronymus (741-75) advanced in his conquest of Slavonia as far as Berea, to the S. of Thessalonica, which is evident from an inspection of the frontiers of the empire, made by order of the Empress Irene in 783. The Emperor Michael III. (842-67) sent an army against the Slavonians of the Peloponnesus, which conquered them all with the exception of the Melugi and Eseritoe, who inhabited Lacedæmonia and Elis, and they were all finally subjugated by the Emperor Basilicus I., or the Macedonian (867-86), after which the Christian religion and Greek civilisation completely Hellenised them, as their brethren on the Baltic were Germanised.[E] That the Latin faith subsequently obtained a permanent footing in these provinces, is due to the influence of the Kings of Hungary, who took the Bosnian Bans under their special protection; and thus it happened that the Bosnian nobles almost universally adopted the religion of their benefactors,--not so much from conviction, it is surmised, as from an appreciation of the many feudal privileges which it conferred, since they afterwards renounced Christianity entirely, rather than relinquish the rights which they had begun to regard as hereditary. The remote position of these countries, however, and the antagonism of the Eastern and Western Churches, combined to retard the development of the Papal doctrines, while a still more important counterpoise presented itself, in the appearance of the sect of Patarenes, towards the close of the twelfth century. The sect was founded by an Armenian doctor, named Basil, who was burnt for his opinions by the Emperor Alexius Comnenus, and whose followers, being banished, retired into Bulgaria, where they made many converts, and took the name of Bogomili--'chosen of God,' or 'implorers of God's mercy.' They thence spread their tenets into France by means of pilgrims and traders, who were on their return to that country, and by degrees laid the seeds of doctrines subsequently taken up by Peter Bruysius, and afterwards by Henry and by Peter Valdo, the founder of the Waldenses, and by others in other places. Availing themselves of the various Caliphs' tolerance of all Christian sects, they carried their opinions with their commerce into Africa, Spain, and finally into Languedoc, a neighbouring province, to Moorish Iberia, where Raymond, Count of Toulouse, gave them shelter and protection.[F]

The same opinions were held by the Paulicians of Spain, who, having received much encouragement from the Kings of Arragon and Castile, also disseminated their doctrines throughout France, in the southern provinces of which they met with great success. There they received the name of Albigenses, from the town of Albiga or Alby. They afterwards spread into Italy, where they received the name of 'Patarenes,' as some suppose from the 'sufferings' which they endured, though other fanciful reasons are assigned for the bestowal of the name.

The tenets of these early reformers 'have been transmitted through various sects under the different denominations of Vallenses, Paulicians, Patarenes, Cathari (Puritans), Bogomili, Albigenses, Waldenses, Lollards, Bohemian Brethren or Hussites, Lutherans, Calvinists, and other Protestants to the present day.' No very lucid account of their articles of faith has been handed down to our times, and some suppose that they entertained the Manichæan doctrines of the existence of the two principles, and of the creation of the spiritual world by the good, and of matter by the evil One. Krasinski appears to favour this supposition; but it is far more probable that, with the name indiscriminately bestowed as a term of opprobrium upon all who differed from the canons of the Romish Church, they have received the credit of supporting the doctrines of the Manichæans. This much, however, is certain,--that they denied the sovereignty of the Pope, the power of the priests, the efficacy of prayers for the dead, and the existence of purgatory;[G] while they rejected all images, relics, and the worship of the saints. Whether the advent of the sect into Bosnia was from the Bulgarian or Italian side is unknown; but, be this as it may, it is beyond a doubt that they were most favourably received (in 1197) by Kulin, who was at that time Ban of the province. His wisdom was so great, and his reign so prosperous, that long after his death it was a proverbial saying in Bosnia, upon the occurrence of a fruitful year, 'the times of Kulin are come back.' Both he himself, his wife, and Daniel, Bishop of Bosnia, embraced the new doctrines, which consequently gained ground rapidly in the country.

In obedience to a summons from Pope Innocent III., Kulin repaired to Rome to give an account of his conduct and faith. Having succeeded in diverting suspicions about his orthodoxy, he returned to Bosnia, where he gave out that the Pope was well satisfied with his profession of faith,--a slight equivocation, which will hardly bear an enquiry,--and thus induced many more to join the Patarenes. Hearing of this, the Pope requested the King of Hungary to compel Kulin to eject them from the country, at the same time ordering Bernard, Archbishop of Spalatro, publicly to excommunicate Daniel, the refractory Bishop.

'Never was heard such a terrible curse. But what gave rise To no little surprise Was, that nobody seemed one penny the worse;' though possibly the believer in the validity of Papal bulls, bans, and so forth, may plead in excuse that the curse was never actually pronounced. The King also contented himself with a friendly caution to the Ban, who thenceforward demeaned himself with more circumspection. On the death of Kulin, Andrew, King of Hungary, gave the Banate of Bosnia to Zibislau, under whom the doctrines of the Patarenes continued to flourish. The fears of Pope Honorius II. being aroused, he sent Acconcio, his Legate, into Bosnia to suppress them. So far from effecting this, he saw their numbers daily and hourly increase, until in 1222 they elected a Primate of their own, who resided on the confines of Bulgaria, Croatia, and Dalmatia, and governed by his Vicars the filial congregation of Italy and France.[H] They destroyed the cathedral of Crescevo, and Bosnia became entirely subject to their influence. From that time, until the latter part of the fourteenth century, they contrived to keep a footing in the country, although subjected to much persecution by successive Popes and the Kings of Hungary, and oftentimes reduced to the greatest straits. Occasional glimpses of sunshine buoyed up their hopes, and the following anecdote, quoted by Sir Gardner Wilkinson, is illustrative of the sanguine view which they were accustomed to take of the ways of Providence. 'Many of the Patarenes had taken refuge, during the various persecutions, in the mountains of Bosnia; and on the eve of St. Catherine (November 24) in 1367, a fire was seen raging over the whole of the country they occupied, destroying everything there, and leaving the mountains entirely denuded of wood. The Roman Catholics considered this event to be a manifest judgement of heaven against the wicked heretics; but the Patarenes looked on it as a proof of divine favour, the land being thereby cleared for them and adapted for cultivation.' In 1392 the sect flourished under Tuartko (then King of Bosnia), and, further, made great progress during the first half of the following century. Their cause was openly espoused by Cosaccia, Duke of Santo Saba, or Herzegovina, and by John Paulovich Voivode of Montenegro. So far all went well; but Stephen, King of Bosnia, having in 1459 ordered all Patarenes to leave his kingdom or abjure their doctrines, their cause received a severe shock, and 40,000 were obliged to take refuge in the Herzegovina, where they were welcomed by Stephen Cosaccia. From that time no farther direct trace remains of this important and widely-spreading sect; though Krasinski speaks of the existence of a sect in Russia called 'Dookhoboitzi,' or combatants in spirit, whose doctrines have great affinity to those professed by the Patarenes, and whom he believes to have been transplanted from Bosnia to Russia, their present country.

But this triumph of Papal oppression was not destined to be of long duration. Already was the tide of Mussulman conquest threatening to overrun Germany; and Bosnia, after suffering severely from the wars between Hungary and the Turks, was conquered, and annexed by the latter in 1465. The religious constancy of the Bosnian nobles was now sorely tried, for they found themselves compelled to choose between their religion and poverty, or recantation and wealth. Their decision was soon made, and the greater portion renounced Christianity and embraced Islamism, rather than relinquish those feudal privileges, for the attainment of which they had originally deserted their national creed. Their example was ere long followed by many of the inhabitants of the towns, and thus an impassable gulf was placed between them and the great body of the people, who remained faithful to Christianity, and regarded the renegades with mistrust and abhorrence. These for the moment were benefited greatly by their apostasy, receiving permission to retain not only their own estates, but also to hold in fief those belonging to such as had refused to deny Christ. With the bitterness characteristic of renegades, they now became the most inveterate enemies of those whose faith they had abjured, oppressing them by every means within their power. The savage tyranny which they exercised would doubtless have driven very many to emigration, had a place of refuge presented itself; but in the existing condition of the surrounding countries such a course would have in no way profited them, but would rather have aggravated their misery. A few, indeed, succeeded in escaping into Hungary, but the mass submitted to their fate, and were reduced to poverty and insignificance.

The rancorous ill-treatment which they experienced at the hands of their fanatical oppressors, was without doubt increased by the fact that these found themselves a small and isolated band, all-powerful upon the immediate spot they occupied, but surrounded by states which were implacable enemies to their religion; while the remote position of these provinces, and the difficulty of communication, have combined to render the people, even now, less tolerant than the more legitimate devotees of Mahometanism. That idea of superiority over other peoples and religions, which the Mussulman faith inculcates, was eagerly embraced by them at the time of their first perversion, and conspired to make them zealots in their newly-adopted creed. The feeling was inherited, and even augmented, with each succeeding generation, until it has become the prominent feature of the race. To such an extent has this been indulged, that the Bosniac Mussulmans of the present day not only despise all other religions, but look upon the Mahommedans of other parts of the empire as very little superior to the Christians. The apathy and indifference to progress which has inevitably ensued upon the adoption of Islamism, has made its effects strikingly apparent in these provinces; and although entirely deprived of all those Seignorial rights which their ancestors possessed, the Mussulman population appear perfectly satisfied with the lazy independence procured for them by the produce and rents of the land, of which they are the sole proprietors. The Christians, on the other hand, are invariably the tenants, as it is beneath the dignity of a Mussulman to turn his hand to any kind of manual labour, i.e. so long as he can find a Christian to do it.

The Euchlemeh, or arrangement for the tenure of land, has long existed in this part of the empire, and has worked well whenever it has not been abused. The original terms of the contract provided that the proprietor should give the land and the seed for sowing it, receiving in return one-third of the produce in kind. The commission of which Kiamil Pacha was President in 1853, endeavoured, whilst regulating the taxation of Bosnia and Herzegovina, to ameliorate the condition of the tenant as regards the rental of land. They decreed that he should be supplied with animals, implements, seeds, and also a house in which to live, while yielding to the proprietor in return from 25 to 50 per cent. of the products, according to the more or less prolific nature of land in the different parts of the provinces. These terms were cheerfully accepted by the agriculturalists, by whom they were considered just. The internal state of the Ottoman empire, unfortunately, renders it impossible that these conditions should in all cases be adhered to, and without doubt the tenants are often compelled to pay from 10 to 20 per cent. more than the legal rent. These instances, however, are less frequent than they were a few years ago, and very much less frequent than the depreciators of Turkey would have us to believe. The most scrupulous observance of the terms of the Euchlemeh will be enforced by the Ottoman government if it be alive to its own interests, and the more so that the infraction of it has been, and will always be, turned to account by those who would fain see rebellion and discord prevailing in the Turkish provinces, rather than unity and peace.

In 1860 no fewer than nine Servian emissaries were caught in the Herzegovina, who were endeavouring to fan the discontent and ill-feeling already existing amongst the agricultural classes. That province has indeed been for a long time employed by the advocates of Panslavism, or by the enemies of Turkey in general, as a focus of agitation, where plans are hatched and schemes devised, the object of which is to disorganise and impede the consolidation of the empire. The conduct of Servia, as well as of greater and more important nations, has been most reprehensible, and with it the forbearance of Turkey, notwithstanding the corruptness of her government and the fanaticism of the Mussulman population, has contrasted most favourably. Little wonder, then, that ill-blood should have existed between these rival factions, and that the party possessing power should have been prompted to use it for the oppression of those whom they have had too much reason to regard as their implacable foes. Yet, in spite of these opposing elements, many points of striking resemblance still remain inspired by, and indicative of, their former consanguinity of origin and identity of creed. The most important of these, perhaps, is their retention of the Slavonic tongue, which is employed to the exclusion of Turkish, almost as universally by the Mussulmans as by the Christians. Some of their customs, too, prove that a little spark of nationality yet exists, which their adoption of Islamism has failed to eradicate. Thus, for example, the principle of adopted brotherhood is eminently Slavonic in its origin. The tie is contracted in the following manner:--Two persons prick their fingers, the blood from each wound being sucked by the other. This engagement is considered very binding, and, curiously enough, it is sometimes entered into by Christians and Mussulmans mutually. Again, a man cuts the hair of a child, and thus constitutes himself the 'Coom,' or, to a certain degree, assumes the position of a godfather. It not unfrequently happens that a Mussulman adopts a Christian child, and vice versâ.

In their domestic arrangements they vie in discomfort and want of cleanliness, notwithstanding the post-prandial ablutions common to all Easterns.

The Mussulman females, up to the time of their marriage, show themselves unreservedly, and generally appear in public unveiled; while in one respect, at any rate, they have the advantage of many more civilised Christians than those of Turkey,--that they are permitted, in the matter of a husband, to choose for themselves, and are wooed in all due form. Parents there, as elsewhere, are apt to consider themselves the best judges of the position and income requisite to insure the happiness of their daughters, and where such decision is at variance with the young lady's views, elopement is resorted to. Of the amount of resistance encountered by the bridegrooms on these occasions, I regret that I am not in a position to hazard an opinion. Polygamy is almost unknown, a second wife being seldom taken during the lifetime of the first. Since it is to the expense attendant upon this luxury that such abstinence is probably to be attributed, it really reflects great credit upon the Bosnian Benedicts that the meal-sack has been so seldom brought into play,--that ancient and most expeditious Court of Probate and Divorce in matrimonial cases. After marriage, the women conceal themselves more strictly than in most other parts of Turkey. Perhaps in this the husbands act upon the homoeopathic principle, that prevention is better than cure; for divorces are unheard of, and are considered most disgraceful. Marriages are contracted at a much earlier age by the Christian than by the Mahommedan women, and it is no uncommon thing to find wives of from twelve to fourteen years of age. This abominable custom is encouraged by the Roman Catholic clergy, whose revenues are thereby increased.

CHAPTER V.

Agricultural Products--Cereals--Misapplication of Soil--Tobacco--Current Prices--Vine Disease--Natural Capabilities of Land--Price of Labour--Dalmatian Scutors--Other Products--Manufactures--Commerce--Relations with Bosnia--Able Administration of Omer Pacha--Austria takes Alarm--Trade Statistics--Imports--Exports--Frontier Duties--Mal-administration--Intended Reforms.

The agricultural products of the Herzegovina are wheat, barley, rice, linseed, millet, tobacco, and grapes. Of the cereals, Indian corn is most cultivated, and forms the staple article of consumption, as is also the case in Servia and the Danubian principalities. The little wheat that is grown is found in the northern and eastern parts of the province, where the soil is better adapted for it; but nowhere is it either abundant or of good quality. The best which is sold in the towns is imported from Bosnia. Barley is more extensively grown, and horses are fed upon it here and throughout Turkey generally. Linseed is only grown in small quantities in the northern parts, while the district of Gliubinski is almost entirely devoted to the culture of rice. As the quantities produced barely suffice for home consumption, no exportation of cereals can be expected to take place. This circumstance, together with its rugged appearance, naturally procures for the province the character of being sterile and unproductive, and such it doubtless is when compared with Bulgaria, Roumelia, or the fruitful plains of Wallachia; but it has certain resources peculiar to itself, which, if properly developed, would materially change the aspect of the country, and obtain for it a more desirable reputation. It is eminently adapted for the cultivation of those articles of Eastern necessity and Western luxury, tobacco and the vine. Numerous patches of land, now either fallow or sown with grain, for which they are neither suited by their size or the nature of their soil, might be turned to good account for the growth of tobacco; and such would doubtless be the case were there an outlet for its exportation, which at present, unfortunately, does not exist. Only a sufficiency, therefore, is grown to meet the local demands, and to supply the contiguous Turkish provinces. Three qualities are produced, the prices of which have been for some time fluctuating. Previous to the Christian outbreak the best of these, grown in the district of Trebigné, sold for about 11d. per pound, while the cheapest was to be procured at 3d. per pound.

In alluding to the capabilities of the province for the production of the vine, I might also have mentioned the olive and the mulberry, both of which would thrive. Of these the vine alone, however, has as yet occupied the attention of the agriculturalists; and though it is largely cultivated in the southern and western parts, not one-tenth part of the land adapted to it is thus employed.

The same obstacle which impedes the more extensive cultivation of tobacco, is also in a measure applicable to the manufacture of wine, at least as far as regards its quality. At present quantity is far more considered, and the result is that, in place of manufacturing really valuable wines, they poison both themselves and all who have the misfortune to partake of it. It is only fair to add that one description, which I tasted at Mostar, appeared to be sound, and gave promise of becoming drinkable after some months' keeping. The vine disease, which showed itself some years back, has now disappeared; and the crops, which during six or seven seasons deteriorated to an astonishing degree, have now reassumed their former healthy appearance.

The numerous hills which intersect the province might also be covered with olive groves, and it would be of great advantage to the country could the people be induced to follow the example of their Dalmatian neighbours, who have covered almost inaccessible points of their country with that useful tree.

The climate is well adapted to the nurture of the silkworm, and the mulberry-tree flourishes luxuriantly throughout the province: were these turned to account there can be little doubt that in a few years large quantities of silk might be exported. A few of the natives have reared worms successfully for several years, and the silk thus obtained has been employed for domestic purposes. The disease, which for so many years inflicted such serious loss on the silk producers of Europe, is unknown in the Herzegovina. Whether this immunity is to be attributed to the climate, or the nature of the leaf upon which the silkworm feeds, it is impossible to say, but it is none the less a veritable fact. Cotton might also be grown to a small extent, but the same drawbacks would apply here as elsewhere in Turkey, viz. the difficulty of obtaining, and the high price of labour.

This has been rapidly increasing during the last twelve years. In 1850, a mason or carpenter received five piastres or 10d. a day, while a common labourer obtained 6d. Now the former finds no difficulty in earning 2s. per diem, while the latter receives 1s. 4d. for short days, and 1s. 6d. for long days. The shorthandedness consequent upon the Christian rising, has of course contributed to this rise in wages; but the province was at no time self-supporting in this respect. A large number of scutors or labourers from Dalmatia cross the frontier in the spring, and hire themselves out during the summer months. The decrease in the number of these was, I am told, very perceptible during the Italian war, in consequence of the demand for recruits.

The other products of the country are wool, hides, skins, honey, and wax, which are exported to Austria. Large numbers of sheep and horned cattle are, moreover, annually exported to the Dalmatian markets.

The only manufactures of which I could find specimens were coarse woollen blankets, twist, and carpets. The blankets and carpets are mostly exported to Dalmatia, Bosnia, and Servia. Besides these, a kind of cotton cloth is made in the houses by the women, from imported cotton, and is applied solely to domestic uses, and is not regarded as an article of commerce.

In considering the question of the trade of the Herzegovina, the attention should be directed, not so much to what it actually is, as to what it might be under the fostering care of an enlightened government. And yet, it is not to the producing and consuming capabilities of the province itself that its possible importance in a commercial point of view is attributable, but rather to its position on the confines of the East and West, and to the fact of its containing within its limits the natural outlets for the trade of that portion of the Ottoman empire.

It is, in fact, in its relation to Bosnia, that it is entitled to most attention; and if we deplore that such natural resources as it possesses have not been more fully developed, we have still greater reason to lament that the world is thus debarred communication with the most romantic and beautiful province of European Turkey. It is also the natural route for the commerce of a portion of Servia, whose exports and imports would thus quickly pass to and from the sea. Its value, however, appears never to have been properly appreciated by the Turkish government, and Omer Pacha, in 1852, was the first employé of that power who ever appreciated its importance in a commercial point of view. He appears to have indicated the measures necessary for developing its resources, and for attracting the trade of the neighbouring provinces from their expensive and indirect channel into their legitimate route. The prospects of the province were rapidly brightening under his sagacious administration, when Austria took alarm, and effectually impeded all farther progress by closing the only port adapted for the transmission of its mercantile resources. She thus secures for herself a monopoly of trade, forcing the inhabitants of all the Turkish provinces, in that quarter, to purchase their imports at high prices from her, and to sell their produce to Austrian merchants, who, fearing no competition, themselves determine its price. The object of Austria in thus retarding the development of Bosnia is sufficiently obvious, since that which would be a gain to Turkey would be a loss to herself. And were events so to dispose themselves as to render this probable, she would doubtless find a pretext to justify a military occupation of the country. This she has done on several occasions, and the large force now massed upon the northern bank of the Save only awaits some national demonstration to effect an armed intervention. This is, however, trenching upon another subject, to which I may have hereafter to allude.

Approximate calculations of the trade of the Herzegovina show that the imports amount annually to about 150,000l., while the exports do not produce more than 70,000l. This comparison proves that a very large amount of specie must be extracted every year from the country, for which no material counterpoise exists, since the merchandise imported is to supply the wants of the people, and does not consequently tend to enrich the province. It follows therefore, naturally, that it is becoming daily more poverty-stricken, and in place of advancing with advancing civilisation, it is stagnating or even declining in prosperity.

These imports are computed to amount to about 70,000 horse-loads in quantity, while the transit trade to Bosnia is estimated at 50,000 more. Of these about 10,000 horse-loads are of salt from Dalmatia.

The main source whence these provinces are supplied is Trieste, where large depots exist, established expressly for this purpose. Thither the traders proceed once a year, to lay in a supply of goods for the ensuing twelve months. They purchase at credits varying from six to twelve months, paying high prices for a very indifferent class of goods. These consist for the most part of cotton and woollen manufactures, cotton twist, silks, iron in bars sheets and plates, tin, lead, brass, hardware, glass, sugar, coffee, and other colonial products. Gold lace, velvet, and silks are also imported from Bosna Serai, and silks and some kinds of cotton prints from Constantinople by way of Salonica and Serajevo. Like most semi-civilised nations, the people of Herzegovina are much addicted to showy colours in their dress. Those most in favour are scarlet, green, and blue; but the dyes soon fade, and the cloth is anything but durable. It is invariably of French or German manufacture; is of coarse quality, and is worn next the skin by the country people. In the towns, grey long cloths, dyed dark blue, constitute the principal article of clothing among the Christians, the general character of dress being the same throughout the province. The exports consist of sheep's wool, hides, sheep and goats' skins, furs, and wax, to Trieste; cattle, sheep, goats, pigs, tallow, and eels, to Dalmatia; woollen blankets, red and yellow leather prepared from sheep skins, carpets, tobacco, wine, and fruits, to the neighbouring Turkish provinces. Pipe-sticks are also sent from Bosna Serai, to Egypt, through the Herzegovina, while knives, manufactured at Foulcha from country-made steel, are also sent in considerable quantities to Egypt. All imports and exports pay a duty of three per cent. on their value, and until recently produce exported to the neighbouring Turkish provinces paid the unreasonable duty of ten per cent. This grievous impediment to commerce has, thanks to the efforts of the European Consuls, been abolished, and they now pay the same duty as exports to other countries.

It may be noted, as a symptom of the centralising policy which the Porte is adopting, that the government now farms the customs of these provinces, in place of selling the right of doing so to the highest bidder, as was formerly the case.

Having thus contrasted the actual with the possible condition of the province, we cannot but enquire the causes which lead thereto; and it is impossible to disguise from ourselves, that to mal-administration is primarily attributable this deplorable state of things. Add to this the total absence of all means of internal communication, and we have quite sufficient to cripple the energies of a more industrious and energetic people than those with whom we are dealing. The first object of the government, then, should be to inspire the people with confidence in its good faith, and to induce them to believe that the results of their labour will not be seized by rapacious Pachas or exorbitant landowners; and, above all things, it is necessary that Turkish subjects, even if they are not accorded greater favours in their own country than those of other powers, should at least be placed upon a footing of equality, which is far from being the case at present.

It would appear that the government is really sincere in its intention of making roads through the country generally, and when this is done a new era may be anticipated. In the whole of Bosnia and Herzegovina, only one road has until very recently existed. It was made by Omer Pacha in 1851, and connects Bosna Serai with Brod, a town situated upon the southern bank of the Save. From Metcovich to Bosna Serai, which is the high road for the trade of the country, the line of route is but a path formed by the constant traffic, and, while always difficult to traverse, is in winter frequently closed altogether. It is indispensable that a central high road should be made, and no point could be more advantageously adopted as a base than the port of Klek, near which asphalte is found in large quantities.

Were a good trunk-road established, connecting that point with Bosna Serai, branch roads might soon be made throughout the province. The nature of the country is not such as would render the difficulty of doing this insuperable, and the rivers over which it would pass are already spanned by good and serviceable bridges, the relics of better days. That the expense attending it would soon be defrayed by the increased traffic is acknowledged by all, and we may therefore hope ere long to see the deficiency remedied.

CHAPTER VI.

Government--Mudirliks--Mulisarif--Cadi of Mostar--Medjlis--Its Constitution and Functions--Criminal and Commercial Tribunals--Revenue and Taxes--Virgu--Monayene-askereh--Customs--Tithes--Excise--Total Revenue--Police.

The Herzegovina is divided into fourteen districts or mudirliks, named as follows, viz.:--

Districts Chief Towns No. of Villages in each District Mostar Mostar 45 Duvno Duvno 25 Gliubinski 31 Stolatz Stolatz 22 Trebigné Trebigné 51 Niksich Niksich 28 Tashlijeh Tashlijeh 16 Priepolie 22 Chainitza Chainitza 14 Kolashin 56 Fochia Fochia Gasko Gasko 20 Nevresign Nevresign 14 Pogitel Pogitel 13 [I]Konitza 19

These districts, with the exception of Mostar (which is the seat of the Central Provincial Government), are under the supervision of a Mudir, who is assisted by a Council, a Cadi or Judge, and a Tax-collector. The province is governed by a Mutisarif named from Constantinople, who is subject in certain things to the Pacha of Bosnia. The Mudirs are appointed by the Mutisarif, subject to the approval of the government at Constantinople.

The Cadi of Mostar is a very important personage, and has all the district Cadis under his orders. He is an unsalaried officer, his remuneration consisting of the fees of office, and whatever else he can lay hands on.

The Medjlis, or Council for the province, was selected by Kiamil Effendi, the Turkish Commissioner in 1853, and vacancies have since been filled up by the votes of the majority of their number, subject to confirmation at Constantinople.

The Medjlis consists of about ten native Mussulmans, one Roman Catholic, and one Greek, so that the Christian interests are but indifferently represented.

Appeal can be made against its decision to the Medjlis Kebir at Bosna Serai.

All legal matters are arbitrated by the Medjlis since the abolition of the various tribunals, which were founded in 1857. One of these was for the trial of criminal causes. It consisted of a President, and six members, and another was a commercial tribunal for the settlement of petty commercial disputes. These have both fallen into abeyance; and, seeing that Christian evidence is not accepted in the civil causes, it is difficult to understand how the Christian population could ever have benefited, at any rate by the latter.

Revenues and taxes.--The revenue of the province is derived from the following sources, viz.--Virgu (income tax).

Monayene-askereh, or the tax paid by the Christians in lieu of military service. It is, however, one of the grievances alleged by the Christians, who declare their willingness to serve; but as many Mussulmans would willingly pay the tax to be exempted from the chance of enlistment, the hardship applies to all parties.

Customs, tithes, excise.

The Virgu is a species of income tax, inasmuch as it is a rate levied ostensibly on the wealth of individuals; but, instead of being a per centage on the income, it has resolved itself into a mere capitation tax, and is ill-adapted, as such a tax must always be, to the relative wealth of individuals. A certain sum was arbitrarily fixed upon to be paid by the province. The government appears to have omitted to enquire whether the wealth of the country would enable it to pay so large a sum as that demanded. In 1853, the tax was divided into three portions, according to the numbers of each persuasion, and has been thus collected ever since.

In the same sweeping manner these sums have been equally apportioned to each household, poor and rich paying alike. Thus the Mussulmans, who possess nearly all the land in the province, and who are generally in affluent circumstances, but who form the smallest portion of the population, pay least. The Virgu has been unscrupulously levied, and has given rise to much discontent, more especially among the Latins, who are the poorest classes.

These complain bitterly, and harrowing stories are told of women, about to become mothers, being compelled to pay the tax on the chance of the infant being a male. Such things may have occurred some years ago, but the spirit of cruelty appears to have died out, or is at all events kept in the background by the Moslems of the present day.

The Monayene-askereh was first imposed when the people were relieved from the Haradj. It is levied on males from fourteen to seventy, and was found so grievous, that the Porte has seen fit to direct that only about one-half of the original amount shall be raised. This alleviation has existed during the last three years.

Customs.--These consist of a duty of three per cent. ad valorem on all imports and exports to and from foreign countries, as well as the same amount demanded under the form of transit dues for goods passing from one Turkish province to another. This has lately been reduced from 12 per cent. to its present rate.

The next source of revenue is the amount realised by the tithes. Since 1858 these have been farmed by the government, but previous to that year they were sold by auction, as in other provinces, to the highest bidder. The arrangement was complicated enough, for they underwent no less than four sales: 1st. In each district for the amount of the district. 2nd. At Mostar, where each district was again put up, and given to the person offering 10 per cent. above the price realised at the first sale. 3rd. At Bosna Serai for the entire province. And lastly at Constantinople,--the highest bidder in this fourfold sale becoming the farmer. This system exposed the tithe payers to much oppression, for it not uncommonly happened that the farmer found he had paid more for his purchase than he could legally claim from the people, so that, instead of 10 per cent., 15 or 20 per cent. could alone remunerate him; and this he found no difficulty in getting, as the government unfortunately bound itself to help him. None but the farmers of the tithes really knew what the produce was, so that any demand of theirs was considered by the government to be a bonâ fide claim, and was upheld.

The government was frequently cheated, and, further, defrauded of large sums of money, as in the case of Hadji Ali Pacha; but it is a question whether so much will be realised by the present system, since greater facilities exist for roguery on the part of the agriculturalists, to say nothing of the corruptness of its own officials.

The excise consists of a per centage on the sale of wine, spirits, shot, lead, earthenware, snuff, tobacco, and salt; of tolls on produce brought into the towns for sale; of fees for permission to distil, to roast and grind coffee, and to be a public weigher; also of a tax on taking animals to the grazing grounds,[J] and of licenses to fish for eels and leeches: these are caught plentifully in the plain of Gabella when flooded, and are of good quality.

Piastres Virgu 1,700,000 Tithes 5,000,000 Monayene-askereh 1,285,000 Customs 600,000 Excise 550,000

Total 9,135,000

The above shows that the province yields to the imperial treasury a yearly sum of about 79,000l. sterling, from a taxation of about 8s. per head on the population. The amount may appear small; but when it is considered that the taxes are not equitably levied, that the heaviest share falls upon the poorest inhabitants, and that a great part of the amount is in direct taxation, it cannot be considered light. The burden, too, weighs with undue severity upon the faithful subjects of the Porte, since they are compelled to pay the share which would fall upon those who have rebelled against the Turkish authority.

There is one branch of the public administration which eminently requires readjustment. This is the police force. Ill-paid and badly organised, it follows as a matter of course that it is inefficient to perform the duties required of it. It is divided into horse and foot, and is paid as follows per month:--

Horse Piastres Binbashee (or Chief Officer) 1,000 per month Uzbashee (or Captain) 600 " Tchonch (Corporal or Sergeant) 250 " Nefer (Private) 150 "

Foot Piastres Tchonch 100 per month Nefer 75 "

The Zaptiehs have frequently duties to perform which should only be intrusted to men of honesty and sagacity, and it is consequently of great importance to render the service attractive to trustworthy men. To effect this the pay, more especially in the lower grades, should be increased, and circumspection used in the selection of recruits. At present this is far from being the case, many men of notoriously bad character being employed, and these are driven to peculation and theft for the means of supporting life. The mounted portion find their own horses and forage, is very dear in many parts of the province.

## HERZEGOVINA

CHAPTER VII.

Omer Pacha--Survey of Montenegro--Mostar--Bazaars--Mosques--Schools--Old Tower--Escape of Prisoners--Roman Bridge--Capture by Venetians--Turkish Officers--Pacha's Palace--European Consulates--Clock-Tower--Emperor's Day--Warlike Preparations--Christian Volunteers--Orders to March.

During the week which intervened between my arrival and the removal of headquarters to the seat of war, I had several interviews with Omer Pacha. On these occasions he showed much kindness of disposition, and took great trouble to explain to me the arrangements which he made for the prosecution of the war against Montenegro in 1852, and to describe the nature of campaigning in that province.

He expressed himself much pleased with a map of Montenegro which I had presented to him, drawn by Major Cox, R.E., British Commissioner for determining the new boundary line, but detected the absence of one or two traversable paths, the existence of which I found to be correct when I subsequently accompanied the army to those districts. The map, however, I may observe, is very superior, both in accuracy and minuteness of detail, to any other survey which has as yet appeared.

While awaiting the departure of the Generalissimo for the seat of war, to which he had kindly invited me to accompany him, I employed myself in wandering about those crooked byways, and studying the many phases of Turco-European humanity. That my impressions of the town were very favourable, I am not prepared to state; but I believe that in point of cleanliness it is superior to many. It is situated on both banks of the Narenta, in a gorge which opens out into two small plains, at its N. and S. extremities. The eastern and larger part is built on an acclivity, and contains the bazaar, government offices, and the houses of the traders and the richer inhabitants. The western part is occupied by the poorer classes, who are for the most part Catholics, and are employed in agricultural pursuits. The gardens, which supply the town with vegetables, are upon this side, and the soil is more fruitful, though marshy and feverish. On the eastern side it is healthy, sandy, and dry. The dwelling-houses are generally small and comfortless, indifferently built, and roofed with stone. As in India, they are always surrounded with a compound--for it cannot be called garden--which gives the town a rambling and extended appearance.

The shops are small and ill-supplied, and the streets narrow and tortuous, except the two main ones, which are tolerably broad, and run parallel to each other in a nearly straight course N. and S. They have raised footpaths, roughly constructed, and swarming with animal life, as is to be expected in the luxurious East. There are no fewer than thirty mosques in the town, whose minarets give it a beautiful and picturesque appearance, albeit that the buildings themselves are imperfect, and ungainly in architectural detail. The Mussulmans have a school in the town, where Turkish and Slavish are taught. Girls are, however, debarred this advantage, and indeed no institution of any kind exists throughout the province for their training or instruction. The result is that the female population is, if possible, in a lower state of degradation than the male. The religious and secular education of the Christians is as little considered as that of the Mussulmans. Thus the only place of worship which the Greeks possess is a small chapel on the outskirts, to which is attached a school for boys, which is attended by about two hundred children. Since Omer Pacha's arrival during the past year, a peal of bells has been placed in this chapel. The superstition which prevails amongst Turks, 'that bells drive away good spirits from the abodes of men,' renders this concession the more grateful, and it is only another proof that the Mussulmans of the present day are not so intolerant as they are represented. No restrictions, indeed, are placed upon religious ceremonies or public processions of any kind. With regard to church bells, I may add that their use has always been considered tantamount to a recognition of Christianity as the established religion of the place. In some towns, where Christians predominated, the concession had been made long before their introduction at Mostar.

The Roman Catholics have no church in Mostar. Service is performed at the Austrian Consulate, and also at a convent, about two miles distant, where the Bishop of Mostar resides. This circumstance has led to the concentration of the Catholic community in that neighbourhood. The Catholic school for boys adjoins the convent; it is, however, thinly attended, and but indifferently conducted.

The British Consulate being closed in consequence of the absence of the Vice-Consul, M. Zohrab, who was acting as temporary Consul at Bosna Serai, I took up my abode at a khan overlooking the river. The situation was pretty, and the house newly restored; but this did not deprive it of some relics of animal life, which somewhat disturb the equanimity of the new comer, but which he soon learns to regard with indifference. Descending the stairs, and passing through the stable, which is, as is usually the case, immediately beneath the lodging rooms, we must turn sharply to the right; and, after clambering up some rough and broken steps, we arrive at the main street, which runs for about a mile through the centre of the town, varied only by arched gateways placed at intervals along its course. Against the first of these a Turkish sentry indolently leans, if he be not seated on the kerbstone at the corner. Passing through this we come to a second gate,

## HERZEGOVINA

where the peaceful traveller, unconscious of offence, is angrily accosted. The meaning of all this is that he is requested to throw away and stamp upon his cigarette, the old tower on the left being used as a magazine. Round it a weak attempt at a place d'armes is apparent, Omer Pacha having ordered some of the neighbouring houses to be pulled down. Nor was this done before it was necessary, a fire having broken out a short time before in its vicinity. On that occasion the inhabitants destroyed a few houses, and imagined the fire to be extinguished. The wind rose, and it broke out again, taking the direction of the magazine. Upon this, the whole population took to the country, and the prisoners, who were located close by, escaped in the general confusion. Had it not been providentially extinguished, the place of Mostar would have known it no more. The prison is a plain white house, which does not look at all as if it had ever been the sort of place to have long defied the ingenuity of a Jack Sheppard, or even an accomplished London house-breaker of our own day.

The tower to which allusion has been made is built on the eastern side, and immediately above the beautiful bridge which spans the Narenta, and for which Mostar[K] has ever been famous. The Turks attribute its erection to Suleyman the Magnificent, but it was probably built by the Emperor Trajan or Adrian, since the very name of the town would imply the existence of a bridge in very early days. The Turkish inscriptions, which may be traced upon the abutments at the E. end of the bridge, probably refer to some subsequent repairs. At any rate too much reliance must not be placed in them, as the Turks have been frequently convicted of removing Roman inscriptions and substituting Turkish ones in their place. The beauty of the bridge itself is heightened by the glimpse to be obtained of the mosques and minarets of Mostar, washed by the turbid waters of the Narenta, and backed by the rugged hills which hem it in. 'It is of a single arch, 95 ft. 3 in. in span, and when the Narenta is low, about 70 feet from the water, or, to the top of the parapet, 76 feet.'[L]

There is a second tower at the extremity of the bridge on the left bank, which is said to be of more modern construction.

Mostar is not a fortified city, nor is it important in a strategical point of view. The only traces of defensive works which exist are portions of a crenellated wall of insignificant construction. This accounts for the ease with which the Venetians were enabled to take possession of and burn its suburbs by a sudden raid in 1717. 'The town was built,' says Luccari, 'in 1440, by Radigost, Major-Domo of Stefano Cosaccia;' but in asserting this, he overlooks the existence of the Roman road to Trebigné, which is very superior to anything built by either Slaves or Turks, and places its Roman origin beyond a doubt. Some suppose it to be the ancient Sarsenterum. That it was selected by the Turks as the capital of the province immediately after the conquest, and considerably enlarged, appears very probable, and the towers which flank the bridge were probably built at that period or a little earlier, though the eastern one is said to be raised upon a Roman basement.

Continuing our ramble we pass through another gate, and come to an uncomfortable looking hill. We have not to mount far, however, before we approach an archway, with two sentries, rather more alert than the others whom we have seen. Officers are passing backwards and forwards, looking fussy and important, as Turks always do when they get rid of their habitual apathy. In their small waisted coats á la Française, surmounted by the inevitable fez, they present a strange combination of the Eastern and Western soldier.

The house in the interior of the court-yard is the palace, usually occupied by the Mulisarif, but devoted, during his stay in these parts, to Omer Pacha, the Serdar Ekrem and Rumili Valessi, or Governor-General of European Turkey. In the vicinity of the palace may be seen the flagstaffs of the Prussian and Austrian Consulates, while that of Great Britain appears at no great distance, and in the rear of the clock-tower, which distinguishes Mostar from most other Turkish towns. Let us now return to the main street, which continues in unbroken monotony for something less than half a mile. If gifted with sufficient patience to continue our stroll out of the town, we come upon the principal burial-ground. On the E. high hills hem us in, while the tiny stream of the Narenta comes winding from the N.

During my stay at Mostar the town was enlivened by the occurrence of the Emperor Alexander's birthday, or the 'Emperor's day,' as it is called. In celebration of this auspicious event, the Russian Consul kept open house, everyone who could muster decent apparel being admitted. After the ceremony of blessing the Muscovite flag had been performed by the Greek Bishop, a select few sat down to a kind of breakfast, which did credit to the hospitality of his Imperial Majesty's representative. Thither I accompanied Omer Pacha, who was attended by a small suite. This was the only occasion on which I ever observed anything like display in the Turkish General. His gold-embroidered dress resembled that of a Marshal of France; his breast was literally covered with decorations, in the centre of which was the Grand Cross of the Bath, and he carried a magnificently-jewelled sword, the gift of the late Sultan, Abdul Medjid. He did not, however, remain long, and on emerging I could not help contrasting the festivities within with the signs of warlike preparation which jostled one at every turn, the first fruits, in great measure, of Russian imperial policy. Strings of ponies laden with forage, and provisions for the army on the frontier, passed continuously, and the streets presented a more than usually gay and variegated appearance. Omer Pacha was throughout indefatigable. Detachments of irregulars arrived daily, some of which were immediately pushed up to the scene of operations; others were retained at Mostar; but whether they went, or stayed behind, he inspected them alike, and was always received with marked enthusiasm. I must not omit to mention that amongst these reinforcements was a body of 1,000 Christians, who, however, were never sent to the frontier. Fine fellows they were, all armed with rifles of native construction. These arms of precision are mostly made in Bosnia, where there are two or three establishments for that purpose.

Thus the days wore on; and, having provided myself with horses, and such few things as are deemed indispensable for campaigning, I was delighted to receive a message from the Generalissimo, on the night of the 13th, intimating his intention of leaving Mostar at 8 (á la Franca) on the following morning.

But before I enter upon my personal experiences in the camp of the Osmanlis, I would fain give some account of the previous history of this agitated province; passing in brief review those causes which combined to foster a revolutionary spirit in the country, and dwelling more especially on the events of the last four years, during which that spirit has so culminated as to convince even the Porte of the necessity which exists for the immediate employment of coercive measures.

CHAPTER VIII.

Bosnia--Turkish Invasion--Tuartko II. and Ostoya Christich--Cruel Death of Stephen Thomasovich--His Tomb--Queen Cattarina--Duchy of Santo Saba becomes a Roman Province--Despotism of Bosnian Kapetans--Janissaries--Fall of Sultan Selim and Bairaktar--Mahmoud--Jelaludin Pacha--Expedition against Montenegro--Death of Jelaludin--Ali Pacha--Revolted Provinces reconquered--Successes of Ibrahim Pacha--Destruction of Janissaries--Regular Troops organised--Hadji Mustapha--Abdurahim--Proclamation--Fall of Serayevo--Fresh rising--Serayevo taken by Rebels--Scodra Pacha--Peace of Adrianople--Hussein Kapetan--Outbreak of Rebellion--Cruelty of Grand Vizier--Ali Aga of Stolatz--Kara Mahmoud--Serayevo taken--War with Montenegro--Amnesty granted.

The history of Bosnia under the Roman empire is possessed of too little interest to call for any particular observation; but, considered as one of the most fertile and beautiful of the European provinces, overrun by the Moslem armies, it is well entitled to the mature consideration of all who take an interest in the important question now at issue, to wit, the fusion of the Eastern and Western worlds.

The immediate cause of the invasion of Bosnia by the Turks, was the dispute between Tuartko II. and Ostoya Christich for the throne of that country. The former called the Turks to his assistance; Ostoya, the Hungarians. A war between these two nations was the consequence, and the Turks gained considerable footing in Bosnia about 1415. Ostoya and Tuartko being both dead, Stephen Thomas Christich was elected King, and was obliged to promise an annual tribute of 25,000 ducats to Sultan Amurath II., thirteen years after which he was murdered by his illegitimate son, Stephen Thomasovich, who was crowned by a Papal legate in 1461, and submitted to the Turks. But having refused to pay the tribute due to the Porte, he was seized and flayed alive, by order of Sultan Mahomet, and at his death the kingdom of Bosnia was completely overthrown.[M]

Previous to this, the Turks had frequently menaced the Bosnian kingdom, but it was not until June 14, 1463, that they actually invaded the country, to reduce Stephen to obedience. In vain did Mathias, King of Hungary, endeavour to stem the advancing torrent. The Turks carried all before them, until they besieged and took Yanitza, the then capital of the province, and with it the King and the entire garrison. Nor was this effected in fair fight, but through the treachery of Stephen's first minister, who opened the gates of the fortress by night, and so admitted the Turkish soldiers.

With more generosity than was usually shown by these Eastern barbarians, Mahomet agreed to leave the King in possession of his throne on condition of his paying an annual tax to the Porte. The payment of this, as I have said, was evaded by his successor, although the old national manuscripts do not even allow this apology for the barbarous treatment which he experienced at the hands of the Turks. These affirm that the King and all his troops, as well as the townspeople, were invited by Mahomet to hear the official ratification of the agreement. But, at a given signal, the Turkish soldiers, who had been in concealment, fell upon the helpless assemblage, and massacred them in cold blood, shutting up the King Stephen in a cage, where he subsequently died of despair; and thus ended the Bosnian kingdom. That his position was sufficiently hopeless to bring about this calamitous result, can scarcely be doubted; but unfortunately the tomb of Stephen still exists, which proves tolerably conclusively that his death was of a more speedy, if not of a more cruel, nature. An inscription is upon it to the effect,

'Here lies Stephen, King of Bosnia, without his kingdom, throne, and sceptre, and without his skin.' Of all the family of the unfortunate monarch, the only one who escaped was his Queen, Cattarina, who fled to Rome, where she lies buried in the Chapel of Santa Helena.

After the death of Stephen Thomasovich the Turks destroyed Michiaz. The nobles, driven from their estates, fled to Ragusa; and Stephen, 'Herzog' or Duke of Santo Saba, seeing that Turkish garrisons had occupied Popovo, Rogatiza, Triburio, Tzeruitza, and Kerka, became so alarmed, that he offered to pay increased tribute; when, his ministers refusing to consent to this arrangement, he was obliged to send to Ragusa for his eldest son Stephen, and give him up as a hostage to the Porte: he having afterwards abjured Christianity, received the name of Ahmet, married a daughter of Bajazet II., and was made a Vizier. The Kingdom of Bosnia and the Duchy of Santo Saba from that time became provinces of Turkey, the latter under the name of Herzegovina, which it still retains, and which it had received from the title of 'Herzog' or Duke, given by Tuartko to its first Governor.

The apostasy of the Bosnian nobles which occurred shortly after the Turkish conquest, may be regarded as the only event of importance which has since marked the history of these provinces. The deteriorating effects which have ever followed the adoption of Islamism are here conspicuously apparent; for in proportion as the country has sunk into insignificance, so the moral state of the people has fallen to a lower standard. Nor is this so much to be attributed to any particular vices inculcated by the Mahomedan creed, as to the necessary division of religious and political interests, and the undue monopoly of power by a small proportion of the inhabitants. That this power has been used without mercy or consideration must be acknowledged; but be it remembered that

'Their tyrants then Were still at least their countrymen,' and that the iniquities perpetrated by the renegade Beys cannot be with justice laid to the charge of their Osmanli conquerors. It would, indeed, be strange had four hundred years of tyranny passed over this miserable land, without leaving a blight upon its children which no time will ever suffice to efface.

As years wore on, other and more important conquests absorbed the attention of the Mussulman rulers, and the rich pasture-lands of Bosnia, and the sterile rocks of Herzegovina, were alike left the undisputed property of the apostate natives of the soil. Thence arose a system of feudal bondage, to a certain extent akin to that recently existing in Russia, but unequalled in the annals of the world for the spirit of intolerance with which it was carried out. Countless are the tales of cruelty and savage wrong with which the old manuscripts of the country abound, and these are the more revolting, as perpetrated upon those of kindred origin, religion, and descent. The spirit of independence engendered by this system of feudality and unresisted oppression could only lead to one result--viz. the increase of local at the expense of the central authority. The increasing debility of the paternal government tended to strengthen the power of the provincial Magnates; and the Beys, the Spahis, and the Timariots, stars of lesser magnitude in their way, could not but be expected to adhere to the cause of the all-powerful Kapetans rather than to the transient power of a Vizier appointed by the Porte.

This last-named official, whose appointment was then, as now, acquired by successful intrigue or undisguised bribery, was never certain of long tenure of office, and invariably endeavoured by all the means in his power to remunerate himself while the opportunity should last.

The disregard entertained for life in those times, and the indifference manifested by the Ottoman government for this portion of the empire, often rendered it the safer policy for the Vizier to make common cause with the recusant Kapetans, who were too powerful to be subdued by force, and too wily to be entrapped by treachery or fraud.

But another and more self-subsistent power had taken deep root throughout the Ottoman dominions, and nowhere more than in those provinces which lie between the Save and the Adriatic. 'In Egypt,' says Ranke, 'there was the power of the Mameluke Beys revived immediately after the departure of the French; there was the protectorate of the Dere Beys in Asia Minor; the hereditary authority of the Albanian chieftains, the dignity of the Ayans in the principal towns, besides many other immunities--all of which seemed to find a bond of union and a centre in the powerful order of the Janissaries.' Of all the provinces of the empire Bosnia was perhaps the most deeply imbued with the spirit of this faction, the last memento of that ancient chivalry which had carried fire and sword over a great part of civilised Europe.

But to that same spirit of turbulent independence, the very germ of existence of the Janissaries, and so predominant among the natives of Bosnia, may in a great measure be attributed the successes of the Turkish arms in Europe in the campaign of 1828, an era fraught with danger to the whole Ottoman empire, dangers which the newly-organised battalions of the imperial army would have been unable to overcome but for the aid of the wild horsemen of the West. That the same spirit exists as did in bygone times I do not say; but whatever does yet remain of chivalrous endurance or reckless daring is to be found among the Mussulman, and not amongst the Christian, population.

Towards the end of the eighteenth and beginning of the nineteenth century, affairs assumed so critical an aspect that it became incumbent upon the central government to adopt some coercive measure. Sultan Selim was the first who endeavoured to suppress these turbulent spirits. He was unequal to the task, and fell a victim to their revengeful displeasure. 'Bairaktar, the hero of those times,' was equally unsuccessful, and the imperial authority bid fair to perish from the land; but in those days there arose one who, like our own Cromwell, moulded circumstances to his will, resolute of purpose, fearing and sparing none. But if Mahmoud was stern and inexorable to rebels, he is entitled to more praise than is usually accorded him, for the steadfastness of purpose with which he applied himself to the restoration of system and order, in the place of the chaos which he had himself brought about. And let us not omit to mention the dignified courage with which he prepared to meet the calamities which now crowded thick upon him. With the mere nucleus of a semi-organised army he held out for two years, both in Europe and Asia, without one ally, against the herculean efforts of Russia to overthrow his kingdom.

There are not wanting those who, besides stigmatising him as deceitful and cruel, cast in his teeth that he failed to carry out the schemes of reform, which they consider to have been visionary and unmeaning. But these, while commenting on what he left undone, forget how much he did, and how little aid he received from without. Well would it be for Turkey this day had either of his sons inherited the vigour, the perseverance, or even the honesty of old Mahmoud.

Since the accession of Mahmoud to the throne, Bosnia and Herzegovina have been the seat of perpetual, though intermittent, warfare. Short time did he allow to elapse before he gave unmistakable signs of his determination to effect a radical change in the state of these provinces. With this view he sent as Vizier Jelaludin Pacha thither, with orders to punish with extreme severity all who should show any signs of discontent. This man, who is said to have belonged to the sect of Bektashi, an order of Mahomedan monks, did not live like other Pachas. He neither kept a harem nor a court, and devoted himself exclusively to fulfilling the duties of his mission. To do this more effectually, he used to go about in disguise, visiting even the Christian places of worship, and thus obtaining a real knowledge of the feelings and wishes of the people. Now as he practised incorruptible, inexorable justice, his rule was as popular among the Rayahs as it was odious to the Bosnian nobles, against whose independence all his laws and measures were directed.

Having taken Mostar and Trebinitza by storm, he at length succeeded in subduing the whole country. Although nominally recalled, in deference to a petition preferred by the nobles of Bosnia, Jelaludin was in reality advanced to a more exalted position of confidence. To him was intrusted the conduct of an expedition against Montenegro, which failed; and little more is heard about him until 1821, when he died, as some think, by poison administered by his own hand.

In conformity with a preconceived plan of operations, an expedition was sent in 1820 against Ali Pacha, the most powerful of those who had ventured to throw off the Ottoman rule.

The operations were successful both by sea and land, and at first all appeared to be progressing satisfactorily. But the extraordinary fertility of resource which characterised the old man, saved him once more; and while the Suliots in his pay overran Epirus in 1821, he succeeded in rousing the whole Greek population to revolt. Although he himself fell during the outbreak, the disastrous results which he had succeeded in effecting lived long after him, not only in Greece, but in Bulgaria, Bosnia, and other parts of the Turkish empire.

The death of Jelaludin, and the revolutionary movement which had spread throughout the empire, led to the restoration of the old state of things in Bosnia. The powerful nobles once more resumed their sway, and the

few supporters of the Sultan were compelled to fly the country.

The reconquest by the Porte of the revolted countries, and the mighty change which the iron hand of Mahmoud effected in the internal condition and administration of all parts of his empire, cannot be more forcibly described than in the words of Ranke. He says: 'We must recollect that the Sultan succeeded in extinguishing all these rebellions, one after another, as soon as he had put down the most formidable. We will not enquire by what means this was effected: enough to say, that he at last re-established his authority on the Danube, as in Epirus. Even the Morea seemed doomed to a renewal of the Moslem sway. Ibrahim Pacha landed there with the troops from Egypt in 1825. He annihilated rather than subjugated its population, and changed the country, as he himself said, into a desert waste; but at least he took possession of it, step by step, and everywhere set up the standard of the Sultan.'

# HERZEGOVINA

Having been so far successful, the Sultan adopted a more comprehensive plan.

Mahomed Ali's successful enterprises served as his model from the first. Mahomed Ali led the way in Egypt by the annihilation of ancient privileges, and it was not until he had succeeded that Mahmoud resolved to pursue a similar course.

'A fearful rivalry in despotism and destruction then began between the two. They might be compared to the reapers in Homer, cutting down the corn in all directions. But the vassal had been long engaged in a process of innovation. In spite of the opposition of his Janissaries, he had accomplished his purpose of establishing regular regiments, clothed and disciplined after the European system.' The fact that it was these troops which, after so many fruitless attempts, at last conquered Greece, made a profound impression on the Sultan. He reverted to the ideas of Selim and Bairaktar, and the establishment of regular troops seemed to him the only salvation of his empire. Therefore, on May 28, 1826, in a solemn sitting of his Council of State, at which the Commissioner who had lately been in Ibrahim's camp was present, was pronounced the 'fetwah,' that, 'In order to defend God's word and counteract the superiority of the unbelievers, the Moslems, too, would submit to subordination, and learn military manoeuvres.' The subversion of ancient privileges, then, was the fundamental basis upon which his reforms rested, and to this the destruction of the Janissaries put the finishing touch.

If Mahmoud found difficulty in carrying out his plans at Stamboul, how much more hard must they have been to accomplish in the provinces; and of these, as I have before said, Bosnia was the most strongly imbued with a spirit of independent feudalism.

In Bosnia, therefore, as was anticipated, the greatest resistance to the innovation was experienced.

Upon the death of Jelaludin, Hadji Mustapha had been appointed Vizier, a man of small capacity, and little suited to those stormy times.

He, and the six commissioners who had been sent with him from Constantinople, were driven out, and compelled to take refuge in Servia, whence they returned to Constantinople.

Again the dominion of the Sultan in these provinces appeared to hang upon a slender thread; and indeed it was only saved by the sagacity of a single man.

Upon the ejection of Hadji Mustapha, Abdurahim, the Pacha of Belgrade, was appointed Vizier of Bosnia. Gifted with great penetration and ability for intrigue, he contrived to win over many of the native chieftains, while he worked upon the jealousy entertained by the Prince of Servia for the Bosnian nobles, and thus succeeded in raising a small army, with which he took the initiative in hostilities. Ranke tells us: 'He was fortunate enough to secure the assistance of the Kapetan Vidaitch of Svornik. Svornik is regarded as the key of Bosnia. It seems that the Agas of Serayevo had already conceived some suspicion of Vidaitch, for they were themselves about to take possession of the place. But Abdurahim anticipated them, and Vidaitch admitted him into the fortress.'

A paramount advantage was gained by this. Abdurahim now felt strong enough to speak in a decisive tone in the Bujurdi, in which he announced his arrival.

'I send you from afar,' he therein said, 'O Mahomedans of Bosnia, the greeting of the faith, and of brotherly union. I will not call to mind your folly: I come to open your eyes to the light. I bring you the most sacred commands of our most mighty Sultan, and expect you will obey them. In that case I have power to forgive you all your errors; choose now for yourselves. It rests with you to save or to lose your lives. Reflect maturely, that you may have no cause to repent.'

This proclamation, which may be regarded as a model of terseness and expressive earnestness, had a wonderful effect. Still Serayevo was not gained without a struggle, confined however principally to the citizens within its walls.

Upon gaining possession of the town, the new Vizier carried out to the letter the judgements which he had pronounced against the contumacious. All who were taken in arms were put to death without mercy, and it was not until he had taken a bloody vengeance on his enemies that he consented to make a triumphal entry into Serayevo.

During the feudal times, when the Sultan's authority was more nominal, the Vizier was only permitted to remain a few hours in the capital, whence he returned to his palace at Travnik; but Abdurahim deemed it necessary to establish the seat of government in that very town, which had ever been the focus of feudality and rebellion.

'Thus there was once more a master in Bosnia. No one ventured now to mention the Janissaries. The uniforms arrived; the Kapetans were obedient, and put them on. The whole land submitted to the new regulations.'

# HERZEGOVINA

Notwithstanding the high pressure system adopted by the Sultan, the spirit of rebellion was still rife, and it manifested itself on the first opportunity that occurred.

The Machiavellian policy of endeavouring to hold both the Servians and Bosnians in check, by pitting the one against the other, was of doubtful expediency; and, as the event proved, tended materially to weaken the imperial cause by depriving it of the aid of the Bosnian irregulars, who had acquired a name for reckless daring second to none. The outbreak of the Russian war was the signal for another attempt to obtain the independence of which Abdurahim had robbed them. At this juncture, too, they displayed the mixture of violence and cunning, so essentially the character of barbarous nations.

From every castle and town, the troops marched to the Eagle's Field, Orlovopolie, close by Bielina, their appointed rendezvous. The Vizier intended soon to repair thither with forces from Serayevo. Whilst preparing to do so, it happened that the people of Visoko, an unimportant place about six German miles from Serayevo, arrived before that capital, instead of marching direct to Orlovopolie, as they should have done. The Vizier sent out his Kiaia, and some of the principal inhabitants of the city, to call them to account for the unauthorised change in their line of march. A Kapidji Bashi, who had just arrived from Constantinople, accompanied the mission, and gave it still more importance; but it was unquestionably a concerted scheme amongst the leading men of Visoko and Serayevo. Thousands of inhabitants had already gone, many no doubt from mere curiosity--for it was Friday, a day on which the Turks do not work--but others with a distinct purpose. When the mission angrily demanded that the force should march off forthwith to the appointed place, some poor inhabitants of Visoko stepped out of the ranks and declared that, without money, they were not in a position to proceed a step farther; that even only to equip themselves, and march as far as they had already arrived, some of them had been obliged to sell their children. The Kapidji Bashi and the Kiaia thought that such language was not to be borne. Without hesitation, therefore, in accordance with the principles of Turkish justice, they ordered their followers to seize the speakers, to take them away, and behead them. The order, however, was not so easy of execution. 'Help, true believers in the Prophet!' exclaimed the men; 'help, and rescue us.' All seized their weapons, the comrades of the prisoners as well as the inhabitants of Serayevo, who were privy to the scheme, and those who were hurried along by their example. The Kapidji Bashi and the Kiaia had not time to mount their horses, but were obliged to run to the city on foot, with bullets whistling after them. The furious armed multitude arrived there with them. The Vizier's force, about two thousand strong, attempted for a while to stem the torrent. They tried to stand their ground wherever they found a position, such as a bridge, a mosque, or a house, but were far too weak to maintain it. Only a small number had time to retire into the fortress, where the Vizier was, and thence they fired with the few cannon they had on the lower town. But the Bosnians, with their small arms, did far more execution, singling out their enemies, and bringing them down with sure aim. The fighting continued for three days. At last Abdurahim found himself compelled to think of his own safety. The Bosnians, who found themselves victorious, would gladly have refused him leave to retire; but the older and more experienced among them, satisfied with the success they had obtained, persuaded the young people to let him go. On the fourth day, a Thursday in July 1828, Abdurahim marched away. He took the road to Orlovopolie, being allowed to take with him the cannons he had brought. There, however, he found that the spirit of disaffection had gained such head, that nearly all the soldiers, whom he had expected to find, had dispersed and gone to their homes. He thereupon repaired to Travnik, and was shortly afterwards replaced by another Vizier of milder temper.

The state of the empire now appeared more settled, both in its domestic and foreign relations, the peace of Adrianople having at any rate saved the capital from fear of an attack. What success the Sultan might have had in his endeavours to consolidate his rule in Bosnia, we are unable to judge; since he found an antagonist to every species of reform in Mustapha Pacha of Scutari, commonly known as Scodra Pacha, the most mischievous, as well as the most powerful, of all the provincial magnates since the fall of Ali Pacha. Young, warlike, and of good descent, he constituted himself the champion of hereditary privileges, and as such virtually threw down the gauntlet to his imperial master. Open rebellion, however, was not the plan which he proposed to himself by which to attain the object dearest to his heart--the re-embodiment of the Janissaries, and the establishment of the old order of things. To this end he consented, in 1823, to make a demonstration against the Greek rebels, but took very good care not to render too much service to the cause which he espoused. Thus, too, when he marched in the autumn of 1828 to the vicinity of the Danube, at the head of an army of 25,000 irregulars, it was not with the intention of attacking the Russians, but rather under the expectation that the necessities of the Sultan would afford him an opportunity of procuring the re-establishment of those 'Prætorian guards of Turkey.' The arrogant pretensions of Scodra Pacha were very strongly exemplified in the attitude which he assumed at the close of the campaign of 1829. Having in the first instance shown much dilatoriness in entering the field,

## HERZEGOVINA

he remained inactive near Widdin during the latter part of 1828 and the commencement of 1829, when, by operating in the rear of the Russians, he might have been most useful to the Turkish Seraskier. The treaty of peace, however, had been signed, and forwarded for ratification to Russia, when Scodra Pacha suddenly electrified both parties by objecting to its terms, and announcing his intention of continuing the war. He even marched to Philippopolis, whence he sent a message that he would arrive at Adrianople within eight days. This naturally caused Marshal Diebitsch some anxiety, since he was unaware of the Pacha's real policy, and believed him to be sincere in his protestations of vengeance against the invaders. A hasty summons was therefore sent to General Geismar, who consequently crossed the Danube at Rachova; and having turned, and subsequently forced, the Pass of Anatcha in the Balkans, easily defeated the Pacha, who made but small resistance. This and the approach of General Kisselef from Schumla put a finishing stroke to hostilities, and Scodra returned home to brood over the ill-success of his undertaking, and plan farther means of working mischief to the hated Mahmoud.

The opportunity soon presented itself. Having succeeded in ridding himself of some of the Albanian leaders, the Sultan applied himself with vigour to the subjection of those in Bosnia who were adverse to his rule. In 1830 he sent uniforms to Travnik, which the Vizier immediately donned. This kindled the spark, and in the beginning of 1831 several thousand insurgents, under the command of Hussein Kapetan, the 'Sonai od Bosna, or Dragon of Bosnia, attacked him in his fortress, and made him prisoner. So great was the abhorrence professed for the adoption of Christian clothing, that the unfortunate Vizier was compelled to perform solemn ablutions and to recite Moslem prayers, in order to purify himself from contamination. The standard of rebellion was now fairly unfurled, and within a few weeks a force of 25,000 men had collected. At the same time Mustapha Pacha, with 40,000 Albanians and others, made his appearance on the scene of action. Without delay an advance was made en potence, and it was confidently anticipated that Stamboul would fall before the insurgent arms. But the Sultan possessed both a cunning and able lieutenant in the Grand Vizier Redschid. This functionary contrived to dispense bribes so judiciously among the inferior Albanian chieftains, that they deserted en masse to the Turks, and thus rendered it imperative on Mustapha to take refuge in his fortress at Scutari. This he did in the anticipation of speedy relief by Hussein Kapetan and the Bosnians, who, despite the dissuasion of the Servian Prince Milosch, had already marched to the rescue. Hussein's answer to Milosch, as given by Ranke, is very characteristic of the man: 'Take heed to thyself,' he said; 'thou hast but little food before thee: I have overturned thy bowl. I will have nothing to do with a Sultan with whom thou canst intercede for me; I am ready to meet thee, always and anywhere; my sword had smitten before thine was forged.' More modest and unpresuming was the burden of the song which they are reported to have chanted on the march:--

We march, brethren, to the plains of Kossovo, Where our forefathers lost their renown and their faith. There it may chance that we also may lose our renown and our faith; Or that we shall maintain them, and return as victors to Bosnia.

Animated by principles which would have done credit to a Christian host, these undisciplined Mussulmans easily overcame the Grand Vizier's army, partly, it must be acknowledged, by the defection of the Albanians, who had previously deserted the cause of Scodra Pacha. Had they now pushed on, their independence would have been established; but, unfortunately, what the Grand Vizier could not effect by force of arms he brought about by guile. With great tact and cunning he sent emissaries to Hussein, demanding to know the terms which they required. These were the permission to remain in statu quo, with the appointment of Hussein as Vizier. These conditions he was fain to grant, and so far worked upon the Bosnians by private and official stratagem, that they commenced their homeward march, leaving Scodra Pacha to his fate. Shortly afterwards he was compelled to surrender. Individually his life was spared, but his partisans did not meet with the same clemency. For the truth of what I am about to relate I am unable to vouch, but can only give it as it is recorded by the chroniclers of the events of those times. Projectile machines are said to have been erected, and the prisoners, being placed upon them, were flung against a wooden framework studded with great iron hooks, and wherever the body of the unfortunate victim was caught by them, there it hung until he perished by the terrible, torturing, and protracted death.

The destruction of Scodra's power was a great feather in the cap of the Grand Vizier, who now lost no time in undermining the authority of Hussein. In this he was assisted by the imprudence of the latter, who committed the error of admitting Ali Aga of Stolatz into his confidence, a man who had always adhered to the Sultan, and was distrusted accordingly by his compatriots. Universal as was the partisan warfare in Bosnia and Herzegovina, there was no chieftain who had supported the brunt of so many onslaughts as Ali Aga. His castle at Stolatz, although incapable of resisting the weapons employed in scientific warfare, was impregnable in those times, and against such an enemy.

In addition to the distrust engendered by Hussein's intimacy with All, the absence of any ratification by the Porte of the recent treaty of peace tended to produce discord in the province. Taking advantage of this, the Grand Vizier nominated a new Pacha, Kara Mahmoud, a creature devoted to government interest. He invaded the country with 30,000 men, and finally succeeded, in spite of a gallant resistance, in taking Serayevo, the capital. The perseverance which he employed in a sinking cause did credit to Hussein, who was nobly supported by the faithful and brave Al Pacha Vidaitch, who had no less than eight horses killed under him in the battle which took place before the walls of Serayevo.

Kara Mahmoud established himself there, and deposed in succession all the Kapetans except Ali Aga of Stolatz, who had made his appearance at a critical moment of the battle before Serayevo, and thus turned the tables against his former friend, Hussein Pacha.

Having thus far succeeded in his undertaking, Redschid Pacha turned his attention to Montenegro, which had been the source of chronic heartburnings since 1804. The nature of the country, and the want of organisation in the Turkish forces, however, once more enabled the mountaineers successfully to repel the invaders. A more important expedition against them was in contemplation, when the Egyptian war broke out, and the services of the Grand Vizier and his army were required to combat their former ally, Ibrahim Pacha. Previous to quitting the country, the Grand Vizier promulgated an amnesty to all those refugees who had fled into Austria, except Hussein Kapetan, Ali Vidaitch, and Kruppa Kapetan. A firman was subsequently given, permitting even these to return to Turkey, although interdicting their residence in Bosnia. On arriving at Constantinople they received their pardon, and Ali Vidaitch returned to Bosnia; Hussein's fate is more uncertain. From that time until 1849 order prevailed in Bosnia, although, as subsequent events proved, a rebellious spirit still existed amongst the more important chieftains, with whom personal aggrandisement took precedence of the interests of the Sultan, their sovereign.

CHAPTER IX.

Hussein Pacha--Tahir Pacha--Polish and Hungarian Rebellions--Extends to Southern Slaves--Congress convened--Montenegrins overrun Herzegovina--Arrival of Omer Pacha--Elements of Discord--Rising in Bulgaria put down by Spahis--Refugees--Ali Rizvan Begovitch--Fall of Mostar, and Capture of Ali--His suspicious Death--Cavass Bashee--Anecdote of Lame Christian--Omer Pacha invades Montenegro--Successes--Austria interferes--Mission of General Leiningen--Battle of Grahovo--Change of Frontier--Faults of new Boundary.

And so time wore on, and Bosnia enjoyed a kind of fitful repose. There and in Herzegovina the feudal system had lost much of its primeval vigour, although a barbarous independence still prevailed, more especially in the latter province, where Ali Aga of Stolatz showed symptoms of forsaking the treacherous fidelity which had secured for him his high position. Whatever feeling of disaffection might have been cherished, either in Bulgaria or Bosnia, was effectually checked: in the former by the judicious tyranny of Hussein, Vizier of Widdin, in the latter by the iron yoke of Tahir Pacha, who fully entered into the Sultan's projects for reform.

The social condition of these two provinces rendered necessary a certain variety in the policy of their rulers. Thus, while Hussein may be regarded as the apostle of political Islamism in Europe, Tahir endeavoured to introduce the European element. He consequently identified himself, to a dangerous extent, with the Christian population, abolishing forced labour, equalising the taxes, and effecting other reforms calculated to upset the old, and establish the Nisame Jedid, or new order of things.

At this juncture the flames of revolutionary war broke forth in Poland and Hungary. The proximity of these countries, and the affinity of their Slavonic origin, could not fail to disseminate the same spirit on the southern bank of the Save. A wild enthusiasm took possession of both Serbs[N] and Bulgares, before which the aged and decrepid Viziers felt themselves powerless.

If it be difficult to realise the position of the Sultan, who thus found himself at variance with his Christian subjects in Bulgaria, and his Bosnian Spahis, the attitude assumed by these factions is equally incomprehensible. Blinded by one insane desire to throw off their allegiance to the Sultan, they espoused the Russo-Austrian cause, demanding their annexation to some Slave country. Thus, by a clever stroke of policy, Austria contrived to secure to herself the cooperation of both the Hungarian and Serb Slaves. And here we may note a curious coincidence, which still farther complicated matters. Whatever may have been their prejudices against the Slavonic Christians, the Bosnian Spahis found it expedient to demand the assistance, not only of the Servians, but of the Montenegrins, the most implacable of foes to the Turkish rule. These at first appeared likely to respond to the summons.

So numerically strong, and so complete, were the preparations for war made by the Bosnians, that, when they took the field under Ali Kieditch, Tahir found it impossible to stem the torrent of rebellion. Never did the prospects of the Porte wear so gloomy an aspect, for there were ranged against it all classes of Slaves and Bulgares, irrespective of religion or denomination. As a last resource government convened a Congress, comprising representatives of all classes of subject Slaves. As might have been supposed, little unanimity prevailed in their counsels, and no tangible advantages were thereby attained. And now a combination of unforeseen circumstances conspired to rescue the Porte from the pressing danger which threatened it. The neutrality preserved by Servia, or rather its Prince, Alexander Guirgievitch, infected not only the Bulgarian Christians, but even the Montenegrins themselves, who actually overran Herzegovina and a portion of the Bosnian frontier during the absence of the Mussulman Spahis of those districts. Undaunted however, by these mishaps, the members of the Congress returned to their homes; and, although powerless to act in concert, succeeded so well in stirring up a feeling of animosity against the government, that the spring of 1850 found the malcontents in a better position than ever for the renewal of the war. But rebellion had now reached its culminating point, and the sudden appearance of Omer Pacha, who threw himself with impetuous daring into the heart of Bosnia, gave a very different colouring to events. To form a just estimate of the difficulties which

he had to overcome, ere order could be re-established in this confused chaos, it is necessary briefly to recapitulate the various conflicting elements, revolutionary and otherwise, which had been brought into play, the aim and inevitable result of which must have been the utter destruction of this unhappy empire.

There are those who profess to believe that Russia has no malevolent designs upon Turkey, and who bring forward many plausible reasons in support of their opinion; but this number has very materially diminished since the disclosures which preceded the late Russian war. The character of the Turkish people, their religion, and their social and political institutions, may all have tended to produce the calamitous state of affairs. Yet when we probe the matter to the bottom, there we find the root of all evil--Russian policy and imperial ambition. It is not to say that this monarch or that was desirous of annexing by conquest, and holding by force of arms, a gigantic empire. Such a thought were madness. Far more subtle is the scheme which was, and is, inherent in every Russian ruler. It has been, and still is, their own aggrandisement, direct or indirect, based upon the ruins of Turkey. Ably and laboriously have they worked to effect that which still seems as distant as ever. No sooner were the bloody days of 1828-9 past, than they applied themselves afresh to the work of disorganisation, and in this appeared to succeed too well. They had launched the Slave against the Turk, and then the Christian Slave against the Mussulman Slave, whilst at the same time the Asiatic Turk--the Turk pur sang--was struggling throughout Anatolia against the reformed and European Turk. It now remained to find a pretext to justify her in effecting an armed intervention, that cloak for so much that is arbitrary and aggressive. This was soon found in an insignificant rising of the Bulgarians, brought on by her roubles lavishly dispensed by old Milosch Obrenovitch, the ejected Servian Prince, and the sympathy felt for Kossuth and Dembinski, who had taken refuge at Widdin. This rising, however, which was at first directed only against the Turkish Spahis or landowners, soon acquired more important dimensions, and on January 8, 1850, the three Nahias of Widdin, Belgradchitch, and Verkovats, were under arms. Having failed in an attack upon the fortress of Belgradchitch, they retired and entrenched themselves at different spots in the adjacent country. Better armed and provisioned, and of greater physical courage, the Spahis soon succeeded in overcoming these disorganised masses, and bloody was the vengeance which they took.

'Victors in every encounter,' says Cyprien Robert, 'the Mussulman Spahis began to visit on horseback the villages, more than two hundred in number, which had taken part in the insurrection. The devastation that ensued was worthy of the most barbarous time. Neither age nor sex was spared. All the young were carried off to the vulture-nests of the Spahis of the Balkan. In vain did Redschid Pacha enjoin milder measures; neither he nor the Sultan could check these bloodthirsty tigers. There needed to that end the unexpected arrival of Omer Pacha at Nish. He fell among them like a thunderbolt, and all was silence. The Bulgarians ceased to flee, the Spahis to pursue, and, what was more, the Russian army of Wallachia halted at the moment it was about to cross the Danube. That terrible Omer, the queller of so many revolts, had at Bucharest an opportunity of making his qualities felt by the Russian Generals, and they were completely disconcerted by his sudden arrival at Nish, when they thought he was hemmed in by the insurgent Serba in the gorges of Bosnia, without the means of making his way through them. The Russian troops paused, awaiting fresh orders from St. Petersburg: orders came, and the whole scheme was quashed. Cleverly as the Russian plot had been laid, it was completely baffled by the rapidity of Omer Pacha's movement.' Once again order was re-established. Serayevo was again made the seat of the provincial government, and numerous reforms were brought into force, all of which tended to ameliorate the condition of the Christian population.

Such of the chieftains as refused to make their submission were pursued without mercy, until the province became too hot to hold them. A few, too proud or too obstinate to yield, took refuge in the Herzegovina, where Ali Rizvan Begovitch, then an old man, opened his fortresses to them. But all resistance was vain before the iron will and temperate judgement of Omer. Mostar fell, and old Ali was made a prisoner and sent in chains to Serayevo. That place he never reached, for he was shot, accidentally it is alleged, by a Turkish soldier while on his way thither. The circumstances of his death will hardly bear an enquiry, and do not reflect much credit on the successful Omer, to whom the blame, as well as the glory he acquired in all else, must attach. It is true that the old tyrant fully deserved his fate, since even to this day the enormities which he committed are well remembered. The old tower on the Narenta at Mostar used to look grim with the distorted heads of the prisoners whom he had captured on the Montenegrin frontier. The habit of decapitating the dead was revolting enough, but this aged sinner was not satisfied with that: he used to drive sharp wooden poles through their living bodies, and then leave them to die a lingering and agonising death. Some are said to have survived their impalement as much as forty-eight hours. The example set by the Pacha was readily followed by those about him. Numerous are the tales of murder done by his followers, one of whom vied with his master in deeds of murder and ferocity. This man, the Cavass Bashee, lived entirely by plunder and rapine. A spot was pointed out to me in the valley of the Drechnitza where a Christian was killed by him while stooping down to drink. I also heard an amusing anecdote regarding him, when he was completely outwitted by a poor lame Christian. The latter was riding through a river, where the stream was somewhat rapid. On the river's bank he was overtaken by the Cavass Bashee, who allowed him to reach the middle of the stream, when he ordered him to dismount, threatening to shoot him if he did not comply. In vain he pleaded his lameness; the ruffian was obdurate. Nothing remained but to obey. This he did, and with difficulty reached the opposite bank. The Mussulman followed, but scarcely had he reached the deep water when the Christian, who carried a pistol concealed, drew it, and, aiming at his persecutor, ordered him to dismount under pain of death. So aghast was he at this audacious effrontery, that he not only obeyed, but departed without farther comment, leaving the Christian master of the field. Whether he took warning from Ali Pacha's fate is unknown, but he certainly died in the odour of sanctity, after performing a pilgrimage to Mecca.

Having thus established the power of the Sultan in both provinces, as well as in Bulgaria, Omer Pacha turned his attention to the Montenegrins, whose incursions into the Herzegovina were becoming frequent and audacious. Penetrating the country from two converging points, he defeated the mountaineers on every occasion, who found that they had a very different foe to contend with from those to whom they had been accustomed. Already had he advanced close upon

Cettigne, the capital, when the Austrian government interfered. Operations were suspended, and General Leiningen proceeded to Constantinople, where he demanded the total withdrawal of the Turkish forces. This was acceded to, and Turkey thus lost the hold which it had acquired upon the lawless Montenegrins. The idea of Ottoman decay acquired daily fresh strength, and a maudlin sentimentality was excited in behalf of these Christian savages. Taking advantage of this, they made constant forays across the border, stirring up by their example such of the borderers as were disposed to rise, and using force to compel those who would have preferred a quiet existence under the Turkish rule.

Such was the position of affairs when the battle of Grahovo took place on May 13, 1858. Although the affair has been grossly exaggerated, and the blame wrongfully imputed to Hussein Pacha, the military Commander of the Ottoman forces, it cannot be gain-said that the Turkish power was much weakened by the event, and the arrogance of the Christians proportionately increased, while the change of frontier to which it conduced tended rather to aggravate than diminish the evil. The new boundary line was defined by an European mixed commission, which decided on increasing Montenegro by the annexation of territory on the western frontier, including Grahovo, which they had held since Hussein Pacha's disaster. Whether the new frontier is calculated to promote a pacific settlement of the question admits of debate, as the province is penetrated almost to the centre by Turkish territory on either side: this, if it give the latter the advantage in a military point of view, exposes the occupants of the country, flanked by the Montenegrin mountains, to constant visits from their unwelcome neighbours, who dash down, kill, burn, and carry off all that they can lay hands on, and retreat to their fastnesses before the arrival of succour.

## CHAPTER X.

Insurrection of Villagers--Attack Krustach--Three Villages burnt--Christian Version--Account given by Dervisch Pacha--Deputation headed by Pop Boydan--Repeated Outrages by Rebels--Ali Pacha of Scutari--His want of Ability--Greek Chapels sacked--Growth of Rebellion--Omer Pacha restored to Favour--Despatched to the Herzegovina--Proclamation--Difficulties to be encountered--Proposed Interview between Omer Pacha and Prince of Montenegro--Evaded by the Prince--Omer Pacha returns to Mostar--Preparations for Campaign.

We now arrive at that period when rebellion actually broke out among the Christians of the Herzegovina, and when things, in short, assumed the aspect which they now wear.

Before entering upon any account of the various risings which have occurred, I would remark that much blame attaches itself to the Porte, not only because of long years of misgovernment, but also on account of the supineness shown by its officials, who, in the presence of the most positive proofs to the contrary, treated the idea of a rising with supercilious disregard. Frequently whole villages came in to declare that they should be compelled to rise, unless they received protection and support. This was of course promised liberally, but the promises were never redeemed, and so they were driven to rebellion against their will, as a means of safety from the fanatical fury of their lawless co-religionists.

After two years of indecisive skirmishing, in which the Turks, always exposed in small parties, generally fared the worst, the Ottoman government appeared to awake to the necessity for pursuing more energetic measures. This resolution was hastened by the revolt of the villagers of Yassenik, Lipneh, Garevo, Kazantzi, Doulatchi, Vralkovitch, Golia, Krustach, Beronschitzi, Yenevitza, Danitzi, and others in the neighbourhood of Gasko, who joined bands of Uskoks, with whom and the Montenegrins they attacked the blockhouse of Krustach. As a punishment, three of these were burnt by the Turkish troops. The version of the affair given by the opposing parties varies considerably, as may be supposed. The Christians affirm that, after repeated acts of aggression on the part of the Bashi Bazouks, they took refuge in the mountains, but returned thence on being promised protection. That they were one day astonished by perceiving the heights covered with soldiers, who entered and sacked the village of Beronschitzi. No blood was shed, but the six sons of one Simon Gregorovitch were taken before Ali Pacha, who ordered them to instant execution. The seventh son is reported to have been taken to Metokhia, where, after being tortured, he was executed. The people escaped from Yassenik and Yenevitza, but in the former two women are said to have been killed and thrown into the flames of the burning houses.

The whole of these villagers affirm that their only crime consisted in having united with other villagers in posting videttes, to give warning of the approach of Bashi Bazouks and Uskoks.

This somewhat improbable story is denied by Dervisch Pacha, who gives the following account of the matter:--The occupants of twenty-one different villages revolted in the spring of 1859, and interrupted the communications between Gasko and Niksich and Grasko and Mostar. They then attacked those villages occupied by Mussulmans in the plain of Gasko, and made raids into the district of Stolatz, from which they carried off 6,000 head of cattle, the property of the Roman Catholics of that district. They further compelled many Christians to join in the revolt, who would otherwise have remained quiet. Dervisch Pacha therefore sent Ali Riza Pacha, a General of Brigade, to restore order. He, after taking and garrisoning Krustach, advised the rebels to send deputies, to show the nature of the grievances of which they complained. These were sent accordingly, headed by one Pop Boydan, a priest, and a leading mover of the insurrection; but in place of lodging any complaints, the delegates appeared rather in the light of suppliants demanding pardon and favour. Meanwhile the villagers returned, but not to live peaceably--merely with the view of getting in their crops.

While the deputation, however, was at Nevresign, the villages of Lipneh, Samabor, Yassenik, Yenevitza, and Beronschitzi revolted again, and cut off the communications between Gasko, Krustach, and Niksich. They also posted guards along a line of frontier, which they said that no Turk should pass. When called to account by Dervisch Pacha for this breach of faith, the deputies replied that the Christians acted through fear, which feeling was taken advantage of by a few evil-disposed persons for their own ends. They, however, undertook to pacify them, and wrote a letter professedly with that object, but without effect. The disorder increased, and numerous outrages were committed. Seven soldiers were murdered whilst cutting wood about four miles from Metokhia; Ali Pacha's aide-de-camp and five soldiers were cut to pieces between

Niksich and Krustach, and seven other Mussulmans were killed. Still the Turks hesitated to act with severity. They appealed again to the deputies, who wrote another letter, which, as the bearers of it affirmed, only enraged the rebels, who tore it, and trod it under foot. But this affords little proof of the intensity of their feelings, as it has since transpired that an arrangement had been made by the deputies that all letters written voluntarily and in sincerity should bear a private mark; and the letter in question was not so distinguished. Upon the discovery of their treachery the deputies were imprisoned, and energetic measures at once resolved upon. To give these effect, Ali Pacha advanced at the head of a small force, and summoned the rebels to surrender. They replied by firing on the advanced guard. The three villages were then taken, and five men and two women killed, while a few prisoners were made. These last were released, but one died in prison. Such is the story told of the affair by Dervisch Pacha.

It does not appear that Ali Pacha acquired any great credit by his method of conducting the operations. Quitting a strong position in the afternoon, he arrived at the villages to be attacked after nightfall. Having fired them, he was compelled to make a precipitate retreat, which might have been most disastrous, had he been opposed to an enterprising enemy.

With reference to the discrepancy manifested in the two accounts, we may feel assured that both are highly coloured. But the deception resorted to by the rebels, and the simple explanation given by the Turkish officials, would tend to impart to their story the greater appearance of truth. Had the Turks, moreover, wished to avenge the deaths of their soldiers, or to vent their hatred of the Christians, they would have maltreated the people of the first villages at which they arrived, in place of marching seven miles through a difficult country to the borders of a district which had for two years defied their efforts at reduction.

The implication of the villagers in the numerous murders which had occurred was proved by the discovery of some of the Turkish bayonets at Beronschitzi, while they actually made an offer to restore the property of the murdered aide-de-camp, provided a reward was paid for them. They even sent a list of the effects to Ali Pacha, with the sum which they demanded for the restoration of each article.

I venture to give these details even at the risk of incurring the charge of too great prolixity, as hitherto a one-sided account only has been given to the world. Every channel of information, whether it be the telegraph from Ragusa or the Slavonic press, does its best to mislead the general public, by exciting sympathy for the Christians, as unjust as it is undeserved. Even in the affair in question much stir was made by the Slavish newspapers about the death of seven Christians, while, as Dervisch Pacha very fairly complained, no notice was taken of the murder of thirty-seven Mussulmans during the same period.

Another event, which afforded a handle for the ill-wishers of Turkey, was the pillage of the four Greek chapels of Samabor, Dobrolie, Kazantzi, and Grachantzi. This occurred in July 1859, and the case was investigated by the Russian Consul at Mostar, who imputed the act to Turkish soldiers, producing in evidence the fact of a sergeant having in his possession a kind of church vestment. The sergeant, however, did not attempt to conceal the vestment, and accounted for his possession of it in a manner which was deemed satisfactory by the British and other Consuls.

It was more probably done by Uskoks, who gutted a chapel near Nevresign a few years before, or by the rebels themselves, at the instigation of others, for the purpose of bringing odium upon the Turks in the eyes of Europe.

By these and other no less unworthy means was the agitation fostered throughout the province, until the whole frontier became denuded of Mussulman inhabitants, who were compelled to take shelter in Klobuk, Niksich, and other places capable of some sort of defence.

By the spring of 1861 affairs had assumed so serious an aspect, that even the Porte could not but awake to the danger which threatened that portion of the empire, and to the necessity for immediate and strenuous measures. This danger lay not so much in the aggressive power of the rebels themselves, as in the ulterior results which it was calculated to produce.

It required little foresight to understand that the movement was destined to be the germ of a general insurrection of the Slavonic Christians of Turkey, which would lead to the partial or entire dismemberment of her European provinces.

In this dilemma the Sultan's government bethought them of appealing to the only man in the empire who was capable of grappling with the difficulty. Omer Pacha was taken once more into favour, and was despatched to the scene of discord. A Slave by birth, but tied to the interests of his imperial master by the devotion of a lifetime, no more fitting choice could have been made. With alacrity he proceeded on his mission--a mission which required both courage and address, energy and endurance.

He commenced his task by issuing the following proclamation, in which he called upon all to return to their allegiance, in full assurance that it was the intention of the Sultan to carry out the reforms which had been guaranteed by the Hatti Humayoun of 1855.

'What this proclamation is I let you all know.

'His Majesty the Sultan has appointed me the chief of his armies in the Roumelian provinces, and has sent me here to carry out in this mission all the just privileges, which have not hitherto been fulfilled. In obedience to the commands of the Sultan, I have come here to show to you how kind and good are the intentions of our sovereign to his subjects, and to announce without distinction to Mussulmans, Greeks, and Catholics together, the following decrees:--

'1st. Every village has the power to name one or two chiefs as representatives, whom I will acknowledge.

'2nd. Every district has the power to name one or two representatives whomsoever the people of the district may choose.

'3rd. The Christians shall have full religious liberties, and shall be permitted to build churches and place bells therein, like all the rest of the subjects in the empire.

'4th. The Zaptiehs (police) shall not be permitted to locate themselves in your houses, but an appointed place shall be set apart for them in every village.

'5th. The arrangement which has been made at Constantinople touching landowners and the agriculturists, and to which both parties have assented, shall immediately be put into execution.

'6th. The taxes shall be collected by your own chiefs, and consigned by them to the officers sent by our Sultan to receive them.

'7th. I will further recommend to the Greek Patriarch at Constantinople that a Bishop of your own nation should be nominated, who knows your language and customs.

'8th. I will take such measures as shall secure you the right of purchasing landed property.

'When this proclamation shall have been promulgated to you, and you should still have some farther favour to ask at my hands, you may do so in writing, or by word of mouth. All that is possible for your welfare I will endeavour to fulfill.

'Furthermore, it is your bounden duty to submit yourselves to your sovereign, and to show humility to him. 'From the Divan Marshal &c. &c. &c. &c. --at Mostar.

'When you shall have heard what I have promised, see that everyone know of it, and what is necessary to execute let me know, and it shall be fulfilled.'

This proclamation, was disseminated in all the Nahias (districts), towns, and villages, and in many instances produced a favourable result. But it could not be expected that these assurances, even though they should have reached them, could have made much impression on a set of lawless brigands, who loved plunder for plunder's sake, and who were supported both morally and practically by the agents of civilised European powers.

Having allowed a sufficient time to elapse for all to make their submission, it now remained to employ force where it was requisite. But the difficulties which Omer Pacha had to encounter were prodigious. An unprecedented drought rendered an unusually sterile country more incapable than ever of sustaining life, while the period which generally elapses between the autumn rains and the killing frosts of winter, renders the time available for military operations short and uncertain. Add to this, the total want of provisions, stores, and other necessaries, which his predecessors had neglected to procure, and an empty treasury, and we may not be surprised that his mission is as yet uncompleted. But another and still greater difficulty presented itself to him. This related to the attitude which he should assume towards Montenegro.

The shortest and most efficient line to pursue, in order to arrive at the root of the evil, would have been to have invaded and subjugated that province. But even had he felt confident of his power to effect it, he remembered too well the lesson of former years, when his successful advance was checked by political interference. There was little reason to suppose that the same power, which then intervened, would allow him greater latitude in the present instance. The idea, therefore, was discarded, and endeavours were made to bring about a pacific understanding, which should result in the re-establishment of order. A meeting between Omar Pacha and the Prince of Montenegro was consequently agreed upon at a point close to the Lake of Scutari. Omer Pacha, accompanied by the European commission, travelled to the spot. All appeared to be going well. Though nothing definite was ever promulgated, there is good reason to believe that the Turkish Plenipotentiary would have offered the most advantageous terms to the Prince, including an accession of territory to the NW. and W., and the possession of Spizza, a seaport, had the meeting taken place. But at the last moment the Prince evaded his share of the arrangement, on the shallow excuse that his people would not permit him to cross his own frontier. He well knew that the Sultan's representative would not demean himself by pandering to the caprices of one by rights a subject, and that the only way in which Omer Pacha would ever pass into Montenegro would be at the head of his soldiers.

In vain did the European Commissioners try to change his decision. In vain they asserted the sincerity of the Sultan, and the safety with which he might fulfill his agreement. They could only elicit a surly, 'Faites comprendre ces gens-là.' The indignant 'C'est assez, Monsieur,' of the French Commissioner brought the interview to an abrupt conclusion. The rejection, for such it must be deemed, of the Turkish overtures, together with the boast which escaped the Prince, that he could pacify the frontier in fourteen days, are quite sufficient proofs of his implication in the disturbances, and would fully justify the Turks, were they to sweep this nest of hornets from the face of the earth.

The Commissioners now saw that nothing more could be done save by force of arms, and were dissolved accordingly.

Omer Pacha returned to Mostar to continue his preparations for carrying on hostilities, not against the Montenegrins, but against the rebellious Christians on the Turkish side of the frontier.

CHAPTER XI.

Leave Mostar for the Frontier--Mammoth Tombstones--Stolatz--Castle and Town--Christian Shopkeeper--Valley of the Stolatz--Disappearance of River--Temporary Camp--My Dalmatian Servant--Turkish Army Doctors--Numerical Force of the Turks--Health of the Army--Bieliki--Decapitation of Prisoners--Christian Cruelty.

Day dawned on September 14, 1861, on about as cheerless a prospect as can well be imagined. A chilly drizzle, swept hither and thither by strong gusts of wind, did not tend to enhance the beauty of the surrounding country, while it portended rather ominously for the success of the operations, the first important step in the prosecution of which may be considered to have been begun upon that day. By nine o'clock, the hour fixed for our departure, the wind had fallen, and the rain began, to descend in torrents, defying all precautions in the shape of cloaks and waterproofs. So it continued until past noon, when the clouds cleared away, and the sun shone out bright and warm.

There is little to interest the traveller in this part of the Herzegovina, unless it be the existence of clusters of old tombstones, which occur very frequently throughout the province. About one hour before reaching Stolatz, which was our destination, we came upon one of those ancient cemeteries, which is well worthy of notice from the mammoth proportions of the tombstones. These are, as is usually the case, adorned with primitive sculptures of men clad in armour, horses, and dogs, and decapitated heads; dates are seldom found, but the character of the work and the frequent occurrence of the cross confirms the supposition that they were erected previous to the Turkish conquest. On our approach to Stolatz we were met by a deputation of the country people, and by bands of children sent out to greet the arrival of him who is regarded as the general pacificator. The anxiety displayed by these to do homage by kissing his stirrup-iron when mounted, or the hem of his trousers, was by no means appreciated by Omer Pacha, who possesses very Europeanised views on these subjects. The enthusiasm with which he was received, however, could not be mistaken, and forms an important element in his prospects of a successful termination of the affair. Outside the walls a battalion of regulars was drawn up, and every here and there some detachments of irregular soldiers.

Stolatz is charmingly situated on both banks of a small stream, which are covered with fig and olive trees, and at the northern extremity of the ravine in which it is built is the old castle for which it is famous. This was put into repair by the rebellious Ali Pacha, and was the last position held by him before he was taken prisoner by Omer Pacha. It is simply a rectangular enclosure, with square towers at intervals in place of bastions, and would afford little security against an army provided with artillery. In addition to the weakness of its defences, it is so situated as to be formidable only to the town which lies beneath it, since it is commanded by several points on the surrounding hills, where batteries might be safely erected at short ranges. On the towers and their connecting curtains are many old guns, some mounted, and others lying as they have probably lain for centuries. Some of these are of the time of Maria Theresa, and nearly all were ornamented with inscriptions and designs. The custom of naming guns or giving them mottoes is very ancient and widely spread. I remember seeing a number of Sardinians grouped round a gun in Capua upon the day of its surrender to the Garibaldian and Piedmontese forces. They appeared much amused, and on enquiring the cause of their merriment, I found it to be the result of their appreciation of the motto upon the gun, which ran as follows:--'Ultima ratio regum.' (the last argument of kings), an argument which at any rate told with little effect in the case of Francis II., for the simple reason that it was introduced at the wrong moment. Doubtless some of these relics of Eastern warfare possessed as pointed and applicable dicta as that of Capua, and had I had sufficient time I should have scraped off the mould and rust of accumulated ages, and have copied some of the inscriptions. That they could be fired was placed beyond a doubt by the promiscuous medley of explosions which greeted us, and which I purposely abstain from calling a salute, so unlike was it to everything one has been wont to classify under that name.

Towns and large villages, may be regarded as the Parsees of Turkey. Their shops are tolerably well supplied with European commodities, and their owners are far in advance of their fellow-townsmen in cleanliness and civilisation. Yet, in spite of this, some of the modes in which they delight to honour even the passing stranger are far from acceptable. Among the least objectionable of these is the encouragement of their children to seize and slobber over his hands, the only manner of avoiding which is to keep them thrust deeply into his pockets--an odious custom elsewhere, but here indispensable. Before bidding a last farewell to the house of my entertainer, I must pay a grateful tribute to its comfort and cleanliness. In vain I pressed him to accept some return for his hospitality, and it was at length only in the form of a present to one of the aforesaid children that I could induce this kind-hearted family to take any memento of their grateful guest.

On leaving Stolatz, our route lay in a SE. direction along the bridle-path upon the right bank of the river. During the first two hours, the rocks on our left were quite bare and devoid of all signs of vegetation. Afterwards they assumed a far less barren appearance, being covered with good strong brushwood, which grows down close to the water's edge. The water is itself clear and shallow, and at one point suddenly disappears--an instance of that phenomenon so common in these countries, to which allusion has already been made. Above the point of disappearance, the valley has all the aspect of the dry bed of a river, with its sloping banks and pebbly bottom.

Our force, which on leaving Mostar had consisted only of a small body of cavalry for escort purposes, and some hundreds of irregulars, was augmented at Stolatz by half a battalion of regular infantry. That the picturesque effect produced by these Bashi Bazouks (conspicuous among whom were the Albanian levies) was heightened by the addition of the regulars, in their soiled garments and woollen great coats, I cannot pretend to say; yet let no one endeavour to depreciate the Turkish infantry who has not seen them plodding gallantly on beneath a broiling sun, and in a country which, by its stony roughness, would tax the energies of the stoutest Highlander.

Those first marches, before we joined the main army, were for us, who were mounted, pleasant enough. Taking advantage of any clump of trees which we might encounter--and these were not very numerous--the halt would sound, and in an incredibly short space of time coffee and pipes would be served to the General, his Secretary, and myself, the staff forming themselves into a group a few paces distant.

During these halts children or curious adults would be seen peeping from behind the trees, bent on catching a glimpse of the Serdar Ekrem. I noticed that he never missed an opportunity of conversing with the country people, who would tremblingly obey his summons to come and receive 'Bakshish,' until reassured by his kind tone and gentle manner.

In thus speaking of Omer Pacha's moral qualities let me not be mistaken: I do not wish to infer that he possesses a very refined mind, still less that he is gifted with those elements which go to form the philanthropist; but that which he does possess is much good nature, a long-headed shrewdness, which shows him the policy of toleration, and a general disposition to support the weak against the strong. Thus, if he has been accused of squeezing the faithful subjects of His

Imperial Majesty the Sultan, I venture to say that these attentions on his part have been devoted entirely to those whom he knows to have amassed money by grinding extortion, and thus he pays them off in their own coin.

On the night of the 15th we halted in a small encampment about five hours beyond Stolatz, where tents were already pitched for our reception. Here one of those sights met our view so characteristic of the country, and so unlike anything one is accustomed to see in regular armies. A certain amount of hay and barley had been collected, and, having been warned to do so by one of the staff, I ordered my servant to push on ahead, that he might make sure of a portion of the spoil. On my arrival I went down to watch operations, and vastly amusing it was to see the scuffle which was going on--black servants, privates of dragoons, and staff officers all helping themselves in a manner that would have wrung the heart of the most generous forage contractor or commissariat officer. Here I discovered the sort of stuff of which my servant, a Dalmatian, was made. Some one, it appears, had told him, with what truth I know not, that a party of Greek Christians had lately made an incursion into this very camp, killing several Turks. This, and the reports of a few muskets, so completely unmanned him, that he stoutly declared his intention of remaining awake during the night; and it was only by allowing him to lie in the tent by my side that I could induce him to try and sleep. The abject cowardice of this youth on subsequent occasions gave me but a poor impression of the modern Dalmatian--an idea which was confirmed by the conduct of his successor, who was, if possible, a more pitiable poltroon than Michaele. That the position of a servant whose master was without bed or coverlet was not particularly enviable, I am ready to admit, and many a time did he come to complain of incipient starvation; but at the moment it was difficult to make allowance for these little inconveniences, which were common to us all.

We were now approaching Bieliki, where a considerable body of troops was massed under Dervisch Pacha, a General of Division. The character of the country through which we passed continued the same--stony and rough, varied only by a little low wood.

The last march was doubly as long as its precursors, and it was late in the evening before we reached the camp. Excepting several detachments of irregulars posted at intervals, the country presented a most deserted appearance; and, from accounts which I have since heard, I cannot help fancying that the cause and effect were very closely allied, or, in other words, that the presence of the irregulars accounted for the absence of the general population. The semi-feudal spirit, which was in great measure extinguished elsewhere with the destruction of the

Janissaries, is still rife in this portion of the empire; and it seems to me that more real danger is to be apprehended by the Porte from this independent spirit in the Mussulman population than from the bloodthirsty hatred of the Christians.

About four hours from Bieliki we were met by Dervisch Pacha. Here, again, we found more Bashi Bazouks, both horse and foot, as well as a battalion of chasseurs of the army of Constantinople. On arriving in camp, I was told off to share the tent of a Colonel-Doctor, by name Rali Bey, who received me most hospitably. He is a young Greek, who has served about eight years, having entered as a Major-Doctor. (Be not horrified, O Surgeon-Major, at so unheard-of a proceeding! Doubtless your privileges are far greater than his, save that you have the Major as an appendage in place of a prefix.) The aforesaid Rali Bey was far the best specimen of a Turkish military doctor whom I ever met. As a rule, they are not an attractive set. Almost invariably Constantinopolitans, they jabber execrable French fluently enough, and affect European manners in a way which is truly disgusting: add to this a natural disregard of cleanliness, and an obtrusive familiarity, and nothing more is wanted to complete the picture. Of their professional capacity I am unable to speak, never, I am thankful to say, having been compelled to intrust my constitution to their hands; but, judging from the fact that, on leaving college, they dispense with books, I felt inclined to attribute the singularly small amount of sickness in camp more to fortuitous circumstances than to the ars medendi, as practised by these ingenuous young men.

The sanitary state of the army at that time contrasted very favourably with its condition some two months later in the year. At the first period to which I allude there were only seventy men actually in hospital, the whole force at Bieliki amounting to 8,047 regulars and 2,900 Bashi Bazouks. Of the twelve battalions of regular infantry which composed the force five were armed with rifles, and were termed chasseurs in consequence. At the same time, it is fair to add that special attention has been paid to this arm, and the naturally keen eye of the Turkish soldiers renders their education a matter of comparative facility.

The night which followed our arrival at Bieliki was, I think, the most sleepless I have ever experienced. So thoroughly tired was I, that the deafening crashes of thunder, the forked lightning, and the deluge of rain, which poured in torrents through the tent, might have passed unheeded, but for the mass of minute life, which defied sleep. With early dawn I wandered off, too glad to escape from my tormentors, and went through the hospitals, surgery, and other buildings connected with the permanent encampment. The irregular lines of tents gave a picturesque appearance to the camp, which was heightened by the configuration of the surrounding hills. Far off to the SE. rise the rugged mountains of Montenegro, at the foot of which lies the plain of Grahovo, a spot fraught with disastrous reminiscences to the Turks. Important as that affair was, since Grahovo was ceded to the Montenegrins in consequence, its details have been grossly exaggerated. It is currently accepted that 7,000 Turks were cut to pieces by 4,500 mountaineers, the real truth being that the latter were probably nearly as numerous as their opponents. The Turkish force consisted of two entire battalions and a portion of a third, and, from the impracticable nature of the country, it would have been strange had the result been otherwise than it was. Hemmed in and mowed down from all sides by an unseen foe, the Turkish soldiers lost all self-reliance, it is true, and the panic which ensued must have tended considerably to increase the magnitude of their loss. In justice to Hussein Pacha, the Turkish General, it should be known that the operations which placed his army in this false position were not of his planning, but were carried out in deference to the wishes of the Civil Governor, and against his advice. From the above remarks I would not have it supposed that I am desirous of detracting from the well-merited praise to which the Montenegrins are entitled for their long and successful resistance to the Turkish arms. Their gloriously stalwart frames, and their independent spirit, both of which they inherit with their mountain air, entitle them to admiration and esteem; but an undue appreciation of these should not be allowed to warp the judgement or prejudice the mind. Some there are who invest them with almost supernaturally noble qualities, while they attribute every conceivable enormity to their enemies the Turks. Each of these views is incorrect. The Osmanlis, whether it be from a consciousness of their own decrepitude, or some other cause, appear to have lost the spirit of cruelty which characterised their more successful days; and it is a matter of fact that the atrocities committed by their Christian antagonists in the Greek War of Independence, during the incursion of the Hellenic bands into Thessaly and Epirus in 1854, or in the present émeute, equal, if they do not surpass, anything which they can lay to the charge of the Turks. Travellers are apt to form their opinions upon the evidence of their own senses; and when such is the case, their verdict cannot fail to be favourable to the Moslems: for things seen with one's own eyes will always make a deeper and more lasting impression than the most harrowing details, the scene of which is laid in times gone by.

It may be urged that the want of power has caused this increased humanity; and in part it may be so, for the nature of a people can never undergo a sudden and entire change. But I can myself vouch for the lenity which they displayed when they have had the power, and to wit great provocation, to have acted otherwise.

The incontrovertible facts, too, remain that Mussulman Turkey has been the first to relinquish the unchristian custom of decapitating prisoners, and other inhuman practices, which the so-called Christians appear little inclined to renounce. This will, of course, meet with an indignant denial on the part of their supporters; but it must be a strong argument which can overcome the disgust occasioned by the sight of women without ears, children without noses, and bleeding corpses of soldiers literally hewn to pieces with knives, all of which I have witnessed with my own eyes.

In matters which do not immediately concern England, no opinion is probably entitled to so much reliance as that of a Briton, even allowing for a certain tendency, which he often has, to measure all people and things by his own standard; and for this reason, that he is probably free from all political and religious bias, while we know that he cannot be actuated by prejudices resulting from community of origin, which invalidates the testimony of the subjects of so many other European states. However narrow-minded Englishmen may be in their own affairs, they are generally capable of taking a broader and sounder view of those of their neighbours than any other people. I think, therefore, that it speaks strongly in favour of the opinions which I have advanced, that they are shared by all those few Englishmen whose calling has brought them into connection with these countries, or the still smaller number who have gone thither for their own gratification. To the former class, more especially, I can unhesitatingly appeal, to bear me out in the heterodox assertion that the Christians are, as a mass, greater enemies to progress than the Turks.

CHAPTER XII.

Tzernagora--Collusion between Montenegrins and Rebels--Turks abandon System of Forbearance--Chances of Success--Russian Influence--Private Machination--M. Hecquard--European Intervention--Luca Vukalovich--Commencement of Hostilities--Dervisch Pacha--Advance on Gasko--Baniani--Bashi Bazouks--Activity of Omer Pacha--Campaigning in Turkey--Line of March--Pass of Koryta--The Halt--National Dance--'La Donna Amabile'--Tchernitza--Hakki Bey--Osman Pacha--Man with Big Head--Old Tower--Elephantiasis--Gasko--Camp Life--Moslem Devotions--Character of Turkish Troops--System of Drill--Peculation--Turkish Army--Letters--Scarcity of Provisions--Return of Villagers.

If the past history of Tzernagora or the Black Mountain is deserving of our admiration and wonder, its future prospects afford a no less open field for doubt and speculation. So far all has gone well with her: the manly character of her people, and their apparent invincibility, have enlisted the sympathies of the world in her behalf, while identity of religion and race have procured for her the more tangible advantages of Russian protection.

That the last-named power is disinterested in pursuing this policy is not for a moment to be supposed. The price she has ever demanded for her protection has been one too willingly paid by these lawless mountaineers, an unremitting hostility to Turks and Turkey. For centuries this was open and undisguised on the part both of the people and the Vladika, by whom, despite his religious calling, the destruction of Turks was rewarded as a distinguished national service. Such, however, is no longer the case; although their hatred is not one whit diminished, or their depredations less frequent than of old, they mask them under the garb of a feigned neutrality and an unreal friendship. Thus they protest, in the face of the most damning proofs to the contrary, their innocence of all connivance with the Herzegovinian rebels. Corpses of those who have been recognised as accredited leaders they declare to be Uskoks, proscribed brigands, whom it behoves every lover of order to hunt down and destroy. But none are deceived by these shallow excuses, which ill corroborate the assertion which, in an unguarded moment, escaped from the young Prince, that he would undertake, upon the fulfillment of certain conditions, to pacify the frontier within fourteen days.

This tacit admission of collusion with the rebels is quite sufficient to justify the Porte in endeavouring to overrun the province, and thus trample out rebellion in its principal stronghold. Presupposing its ability to effect this, we then arrive at the real debatable point, whether such a course would be allowed by the other powers. In the case of England the answer can hardly be doubtful; for it would ill behove a country, in whose Parliament all religions are tolerated, to interfere in the matter, abandoning that policy of non-intervention which she has so openly confessed and so successfully pursued, upon the narrow grounds of the inexpediency of permitting a Mussulman power to overrun a Christian province, and a province, be it remembered, which legally composes an integral portion of the Turkish empire.

The candid announcement made by the Porte of its intention to abandon the policy of forbearance towards Montenegro, which it has as yet pursued, betokens the existence of a small spark of its ancient spirit, and augurs well for its success. Should the belligerents be left to themselves, I believe that it will succeed; but the web of political intrigue which has grown around the question, fostered by hereditary policy, imperial ambition, and private machination, render it difficult to foretell the issue. The chances which render success probable are the deference which France has of late shown to the wishes of England, the want of union prevalent throughout the Austrian empire, and the internal movement in Russia, which incapacitates her from doing mischief in this part of Europe. Yet, let us not disguise from ourselves the self-evident fact, that the views of Russia remain unaltered, that the policy of Peter is still maintained inviolate, and that, although the last war may have convinced her that actual self-aggrandisement will not be tolerated, she still holds one object ever in view--the destruction of Turkish supremacy on both banks of the Danube and the substitution of dependent Slavism.

Throughout European Turkey, and nowhere more than in Montenegro, has her influence waned since the Eastern war; yet so long as she shall possess, and so freely use, the golden key, she must and will have very great weight.

Of the three causes which, as I have said, tend to complicate the Herzegovinian-Montenegrin question, private machinations have recently been the most successful, and consequently the most injurious to order and the general weal. The energy of some of the foreign employés has been truly astounding, while their glib tongues and manoeuvring minds have worked metamorphoses worthy of Robin or the Wizard of the North. This distortion of facts was somewhat naïvely described by a French colleague of M. Hecquard.[P]

'Montenegro,' said the former gentleman, 'c'est une invention de Monsieur Hecquard.' Instances of such duplicity have been frequently brought to light. These, while they reflect little credit on the individual, speak badly for the good faith of the government represented, as discovery is rarely followed by punishment--frequently quite the reverse.

The high-handed policy which the Porte is now pursuing is the most likely to be attended with beneficial results; for, as experience has shown us, the system of concession is entirely useless, each addition to their territory only making the Montenegrins the more grasping and more avaricious. That a solution of the difficulty must in some way be arrived at is clear. Should Turkey fail in effecting this by the means she is now adopting, Europe will be called on to interfere; for while things exist as at present, the developement of those countries in agriculture or commerce is as impossible as in civilisation and Christianity.

The disorganised condition of the Herzegovina, with its attendant incubus of half a million of debt, renders it certain that one of two results must inevitably ensue:

either Turkey will be compelled to surrender that province, and possibly Bosnia also, or she will sustain a still severer blow to her already shattered finances. Of the two evils, the latter is the least in the opinion of the Ottoman government, and it was this consideration which induced it to determine on the prosecution of hostilities in 1861. Several causes combined to retard the commencement of military operations until late in the year. The principal reasons were, the almost unprecedented drought which prevailed during that year, and the deference shown by Omer Pacha to the wishes of the European Commission, then sitting at Mostar, whose members did all in their power to arrive at a satisfactory conclusion without having recourse to arms. In the meantime troops were being massed, and stores, provisions, and magazines provided at Gasko, Bieliki, and Trebigné. The country infested by the insurgents extended from Bosnia round the frontier as far as Suttorina, in the vicinity of which Luca Vukalovitch had established his quarters. This man, who has acquired a certain notoriety, was a blacksmith by trade, but, preferring a life of lawless indolence to honest labour, betook himself to his present calling. He appears to be quite devoid of that chivalrous courage which has distinguished many of his class, and consequently deserves neither sympathy when free nor mercy from his captors when taken.

On September 3 the first move was made. Columns left Bieliki and Trebigné, which, after scouring the district surrounding Grahovo, returned without effecting any important results. A re-distribution of the troops then took place. Trebigné was almost denuded of regular soldiers, its defence being intrusted to Bashi Bazouks, while the entire force was distributed at other points of the frontier, Bieliki and Gasko constituting a permanent base of operations. At the former of these Dervisch Pacha was in command, a man of considerable military talent, though thoroughly unscrupulous, while another General of Division, Osman Pacha, had his head-quarters at Gasko.

Such was the position of affairs on September 18, 1861. Upon the morning of that day, intelligence was received of such a nature as to render an immediate move advisable. An order to this effect was issued at 2 P.M., just as I had succeeded in rendering habitable a very smart little tent, which had previously belonged to the Spanish General Prim, and had been given by him to Omer Pacha after the campaign on the Danube. At 3 P.M. six battalions paraded with eight guns, and some sappers, the whole under the command of Ali Pacha of Scutari, a General of Brigade. For some hours our course lay in a NE. direction along a ridge, and separated only by the intervening gorge from the mountains of the Baniani, which ran parallel on our right. These were known to be infested with rebels, traces of whom were found by a force of irregulars sent to attack them during the chilly hours of morning. Here I, for the first time, saw Omer Pacha throw off the air of easy carelessness habitual to him, and apply himself con amore to the work before him. He selected the positions to be occupied by the outposts and picquets, indicating to his staff such points as he considered most worthy of their attention, and endeavouring, by his own exertions, to atone for the shortcomings of his subordinates. The force bivouacked that night on the side of a hill overhanging a hollow, in which was pitched one of the small camps with which these districts are now interspersed. The choice of ground was certainly most injudicious, and the General expressed his annoyance in no measured terms.

From this time the privations endured by the troops were very great. Long marches over an almost impracticable country by day, the most intense cold by night, without tents or extra clothing, and with little food, were endured with uncomplaining devotion. In some measure I could sympathise with them, having passed all the nights since leaving Mostar without bed or blanket. Thus many a cold morning hour did I eke out in vain search for wood to kindle a little fire; and had I to undergo the ordeal again, I should certainly prefer to pass the night á la belle étoile, with my toes to the smouldering embers of a camp fire, and my head well wrapped up after the manner of all Easterns.

On the second day after leaving Bieliki, our course lay due N. through a perfect wilderness of rocks, varied only by an occasional basin, formed by surrounding hills, and covered with a species of dwarf vegetation. The appearance of the force, as it straggled over this wavy expanse of stone, was curious enough, and it certainly baffles all attempts at description; so I must ask my readers to allow their imagination to people the mer de glace with some thousands of Oriental soldiers, regular and irregular, pipe-bearers, and household servants formidably armed, and they will not be far from a just conception of the case. After marching for five hours over this inhospitable tract, we halted at the mouth of a valley where the hills open out into a small plain. This forms the entrance to the Pass of Koryta, whence we had just emerged. It is a spot of ill repute even amongst the barbarous inhabitants of these regions; and more Turks have received their death-wounds from behind the boulders, which have served to screen the assassins, or from the knives of the ever-ready Greeks in that fatal gorge, than in any other spot of these disordered lands. The Pass is formed by the extremities of Banyani and Pianina, and is of much strategical importance. It was one of the first points subsequently occupied by Omer Pacha. Many a disaster has been brought about by the incautious recklessness of those in command of Turkish troops, and it was with some satisfaction that I saw the heights both in front and rear crowned by Turkish battalions, before the remainder were allowed to pile their arms, and betake themselves to sleep or any other recreation. It was impossible not to revert in imagination to the scenes of blood and strife of which Koryta has been the site, as contrasted with its appearance at that moment. Groups of Turkish soldiers were amusing themselves by dancing a national dance, with as much gaiety as though they had not marched a yard, and with far more activity than one would be disposed to give them credit for possessing. The dance, a kind of jumping reel, was accompanied by droning music not unlike the pipes. A little farther a regimental band was murdering the two or three European airs with which it was acquainted. One of these, to which they showed a good-natured antipathy by frequently murdering, was 'La Donna è Mobile,' or 'La Donna Amabile,' as Omer took pleasure in calling it. And thus the day wore on, until, late in the evening, we arrived at Tchernitza, a little town of about 600 inhabitants. Our camp was formed on a level plot, which looked green and pleasant after the barren country through which we had passed. Just above the spot where the men bivouacked was a lofty mound surmounted by a turret, from which an armed sentry of a regiment of redif (or militia) kept watch over the surrounding country. While taking a bird's-eye view from this point, I heard myself accosted, to my no small astonishment, in very fair English by a Turkish officer. My new acquaintance proved to be one Hakki Bey, a Major of Engineers, employed on the staff of Osman Pacha. He told me that, after having passed ten years at the Turkish Military College, he had been sent to England for five years to complete his education. What can the world say of Turkish education after this stupendous example? He was an officer of much intelligence, and soon worked himself into Omer Pacha's good graces. On the following morning I met Osman Pacha at breakfast in the Generalissimo's tent. He answers fully to the latter's description of him, as being a man of much feeling, and very much the reverse of what he is represented by Mr. Oliphant. That gentleman, in his narrative of the Trans-Caucasian campaign, calls him 'a thorough Moslem, and a hater of all Feringhees.' Now I am at a loss to conceive on what grounds he can base that assertion; for, excepting that he speaks no language but his own--a very common circumstance with English gentlemen of a certain age-- he is thoroughly European in his ideas and tendencies. Of his kindness to myself under circumstances of difficulty and danger I shall ever entertain the most lively recollection.

While peering about in the single street of Tchernitza, I observed a crowd collected in one corner. The centre of attraction proved to be a man with a big head. The unfortunate creature seemed to experience very much the same treatment as he would have met with had he been turned loose in the streets of London. Everybody stared, most people laughed, and some jeered at his terrible affliction. He may have numbered some five-and-forty years, stood about five feet four inches high, with a head of about twice the natural size. The idiotic appearance produced by this deformity was increased by the dimensions of his tongue, which protruded from his mouth, and hung down at the side in the most woe-begone manner. The poor wretch accepted the banter of the spectators with that good-humoured indifference which leads one to hope that the victims of such freaks of nature are insensible to the full weight of their calamity. To the SE. of the town or village stand the ruins of an old castle, once the favourite resort of the Dukes of Herzegovina. Nought save the remnant of the walls remains to mark its importance in days gone by.

The remainder of our march to Gasko was in the plain, and presented few objects to attract attention, unless it was another victim of fell disease. A poor girl, suffering from elephantiasis, was one of the only women whom I had seen for many days. Her foot was swollen to an incredible size, and I have been since informed that it is not an uncommon complaint in those countries. As usual, we found the force already encamped at Gasko drawn up to receive us, four mountain guns on either flank. These were mounted, and drawn by two mules. In places inaccessible to wheeled carriages, they are carried, as in our own service, by two mules, viz. the gun on one, and the carriage on the other.

The infantry presented a more creditable appearance than any I had yet seen, and the encampment generally looked clean and orderly. Camp life is under no circumstances a very agreeable phase of existence, and least of all in Eastern countries, when divested of the excitement resulting from the probability of an attack. In other lands there is sure to be something to attract the mind. Staff officers in gay uniforms pass and repass in all the importance of official haste, cornets of cavalry bent on performing the onerous duties of galloper, and the pompous swagger of infantry drum-majors, all combine to vary the scene and amuse the eye. But in Turkey this is not so. All are equally dirty and unkempt, while the hideous attempts at music have very far from a soothing effect. An attentive listener may hear a single voice four times in the day calling to prayer, a custom which, under no circumstances, is ever omitted. Of the internal response to this appeal I am of course unable to judge, but from outward appearance I should imagine it to be small. The Pachas, it is true, indulge in the somewhat unintellectual amusement of twiddling a chain of beads, talking on indifferent subjects the while; but I never observed even this small tribute of respect amongst the inferior officers. And thus the day wears on in dull monotony, until at sunset a crash of many voices may be heard from the centre of the camp, rising up to heaven, and calling down a blessing on their Sultan's head.

Immediately upon his arrival at Gasko, Omer Pacha had betaken himself to the only habitable house in the adjacent village, coming down to camp with early morning. I consequently became the guest of Osman Pacha, who treated me with uniform kindness. It is a strange coincidence that almost every Turkish Pacha, whatever may have been his origin, however low his moral character, possesses a dignity of deportment and a charm of manner which among Europeans is deemed an infallible test of a kind heart and high breeding. This, however, does not apply in its full sense to Osman, for a more amiable and moral old gentleman never breathed. Indeed, I much fear that the good qualities of his heart somewhat eclipsed those of his head, as subsequent events will show. Many of his remarks, however, were shrewd and pointed enough; thus, while comparing the English with the Turkish soldier, he very candidly admitted that the former carried off the palm in the matter of fighting, with the following reservations--that the Turk is content to serve with a very considerable arrear of pay, and with very little in the way of clothing or nourishment; that he is able to endure equal if not greater fatigue and hardship; and lastly, that he does not indulge in strong drinks. All this must be admitted by the most prejudiced arbitrator; nor is it the highest eulogium to which the Moslem soldier is entitled. Habits of order and obedience, which are only sustained in European armies by the strictest discipline, form part of the national character, and therefore render the minuter details of military economy unnecessary. That they will ever become sufficiently familiarised with their European clothing as to present a smart appearance, is improbable; yet their parade movements are even now performed with considerable accuracy and rapidity in the loose shuffling manner in vogue amongst the French, while of their prowess in the field we have had ample proofs on divers occasions--whether in the European campaign of 1828, when, despite the confusion resulting from the recent destruction of the Janissaries, they beat the Russians at all points; or in Asia during that and the following years, where, if not so successful, they often displayed a heroism unsurpassed in history. Or, coming down to the present time, we have but to recall the noble stand made at Kars and Silistria, which, almost without defences, they held for months against the most determined efforts of Mouravieff and Paskievitch. Singularly enduring, brave, and obedient, they require only good leading to form them into one of the most effective armies of the world. But this is precisely the one thing in which they are most strikingly deficient, and of which there is little hope of any permanent amelioration.

In no department of the public administration are the baneful effects of that spirit of insincerity and rapacity, which is almost universal at Constantinople, more apparent than in the army. Money drawn upon the authority of false returns, and eventually appropriated by the highest people of the land, affords an example of peculation and dishonesty which is carried out through all ranks, and the result is that the greater portion of the army has received no pay for more than six-and-twenty months. There is reason to believe that this system of sending in false numerical returns has been of late carried to an incredible extent. The nominal strength of the Turkish army is as follows:--6 corps d'armées, each consisting of 6 regiments of 4 battalions, each battalion numbering 1,000 effective men, with a proportion of cavalry and artillery to each corps d'armée.

This gives us 144,000 regular infantry; and yet I have good authority for saying that, should Turkey enter upon a war to-morrow, she would do so with less than 80,000 regular infantry. Of these 29 of the strongest battalions were in the Herzegovina during the past autumn, and that force has received a slight increase during the winter months. To the merits of these troops I have already borne testimony. Against those by whom they are officered I would now raise a protest, since they appeared to be so selected without regard to any one qualification which may entitle them to the rank. Even were the finances of the empire restored to a flourishing condition, and other reforms instituted, the army cannot be thoroughly effective until it is re-officered, and the new officers duly impressed with a conviction of the just distribution of rewards and punishments. It is deplorable that so low a sentiment should be the only one with which to inspire the officers, in order to secure the zealous fulfillment of their duties. But so it is: their birth and education, and the flagrant instances of bought rewards, which are constantly before their eyes, combine to render it the best sentiment of which they are capable. This applies principally to the regimental officers in the lower ranks, upon whom the efficiency of an army so much depends. Great good is anticipated from the extended scale introduced into the Military College, and it is said to be the intention of the government to appoint as soon as possible officers to commands who have passed through it, to the extinction of the old system of conferring the highest rank upon Pachas, whether fitted for the position or not.

Excepting the chief of the staff, and some of the aides-de-camp, the staff in the field was composed of engineer officers, most of whom had passed some years in France or Belgium, while one had remained five years in England. But these are men of a very different stamp from the general run of regimental officers, who appear to think it the greatest privilege of their position to get very drunk whenever the opportunity offers itself, thus presenting a curious contrast with the remarkable sobriety of their men. One evening I chanced to witness a scene as amusing as it was characteristic of the people among whom I lived. A post had arrived, and Osman Pacha's private Secretary was occupied in dispensing the letters. The officers were admitted to his tent, and the childish glee which they displayed was diverting in the extreme. Not only did they mark their gratitude by kissing every portion of the Secretary's garments on which they could lay hand, but danced about, showing the epistles to all who approached. Fortunately, perhaps, few of these could read, so the breach of confidence was not very great. I have often noticed that an Oriental, when he does shake off the apathetic reserve habitual to him, becomes more excited and enthusiastic than warmer-blooded nations. At any rate they seem to possess a full measure of that natural instinct of joy at receiving tidings of loved ones in far distant lands. One of these letters was from the wife of an officer, who had not heard from her for many months, and whose last reports had informed him of the destruction of his house by fire. The apparent indifference with which he had received the first announcement completely gave way to a flood of happiness on hearing of the safety of those he loved. Verily they are not so devoid of feeling as is generally supposed--these fatalist Turks.

The arrival of Dervisch Pacha with six battalions from Bieliki, which was now occupied by two battalions of redif, converted Gasko into the sole base of operations. The rain, which had for the past few days fallen in torrents, would have enabled Omer Pacha to have commenced hostilities on a greater scale, but for the dearth of provisions, which should have reached the frontier long since. It now became apparent that little could be done during the remaining months of the year, for nature had effected for the rebels whatever the indolence of the Turkish commanders had left undone. The magnificent harvest of the preceding year, which the rebels had appropriated, and the extraordinary drought which had prevailed during the spring and summer of 1861, combined to diminish the Turkish prospects of success. Moreover, the object of the Generalissimo was not so much to hunt down the rebels as to inspire them with confidence in the leniency of the Sultan's rule, while he, at the same time, occupied the country in such force as to convince them of the necessity of eventual submission. Already were the good effects of this measure manifested in the rapid return of the inhabitants to the surrounding villages. Metokhia, Aphtoria, and Lubniak, all in the close vicinity of the Turkish camp, had been deserted by their occupants, who, like the majority in the plain of Gasko, are of the Mussulman religion. These now returned to their desolated homes.

CHAPTER XIII.

Expedition to Niksich--Character of Scenery--Engineer Officers--Want of Maps--Affghan Dervish--Krustach--Wallack Colonel--Bivouac--Bashi Bazouks--Pass of Dougah--Plain of Niksich--Town and Frontier--Albanian Mudir--Turkish Women--Defects of Government by Mudir and Medjlis.

The ennui produced by a long halt after a series of consecutive marches had by this time taken such a hold on me, that with delight I heard Omer Pacha's announcement of his intention to send a force with provisions for the town and garrison of Niksich, whose proximity to Montenegro placed them in the position of a beleaguered garrison, and rendered them dependent upon the government for the ordinary necessaries of life. For this duty Osman Pacha was detached, taking with him seven battalions and four guns, which were subsequently reinforced by an eighth battalion from Krustach. For the first three hours our route lay in the valley of Gasko, which looked green and fertile, though showing few signs of cultivation. The ruins of a church were the only antiquarian relics which I noticed on the march. At the extremity of the valley the pathway winds to the SE., having the rugged Piwa, looking bleak and bare, on the left, and the more wooded heights of Baniani on the right. The configuration of the hills, and the sharp outline of the country generally, combined with the indescribably wild and rocky character of some parts of the foreground, and the sloping grass banks in others, to produce a picture at once grand and picturesque; but it was a picture of which the eye soon wearied and the appreciation palled. There, as throughout the whole march to Niksich, the country abounds with the most magnificent defensible positions; natural parapets, whence a most destructive fire might be poured upon an advancing foe, and incapable of being turned by any flank movement; positions, in short, constructed for the enactment of a second Thermopylæ. No signs of humanity were to be found in that barren region. Here and there the carcass of a stray horse, which had died probably of pure inanition, and afforded a scanty meal to the birds and beasts of prey, was the only sign of aught that had ever beat with the pulse of life. Leaving the main body, I came up with a small party of engineer officers, employed in taking the angles on the line of march. The serious inconvenience resulting from the want of a good map of these countries is now much felt. True, it was partially removed by the existence of a map of Montenegro, including a portion of the Herzegovinian frontier, drawn by Major Cox[Q], R.E., and published by the Topographical Department, a copy of which I had presented to Omer Pacha, and which was much appreciated by him. Very properly, however, he proposes that the country shall be surveyed by Turkish officers, and a map constructed upon their observations. Its accuracy will be somewhat doubtful, if we may judge from the crude manner in which they set to work. The only instruments employed were prismatic compasses, with which they jotted down angles at all the salient points, an orderly dragoon counting his horse's paces in the intervening time, which was occasionally as much as twenty minutes. Passing these I reach the advance guard, and still pressing on I soon find myself alone. No, not quite alone; another turn of the rocks brings me abreast of a strange companion, his long flowing dress of yellow surge, and Dervish's hat, with its hair-fringe, proclaim him to be one of that large class of religious devotees who live in indolence by working upon the superstition of their co-religionists. My friend, however, was a man of some affluence, and very superior in all respects to the generality of his order. By birth an Affghan, he has spent many years in the Herzegovina, and had followed the army for some weeks before I chanced to meet him. Wherever there was a prospect of work or danger there were his little bay stallion and tufted lance always to be seen. There was something weird-like in his presence, as he now sat like a statue on his horse, and anon darted forward with a flourish of his lance, sending up wreaths of blue smoke from the inseparable chibouque. We thus rode in company until we overtook the small force of irregulars, who had been sent in advance of the main body. This constant use of, and great reliance on, the Bashi Bazouks, is most prejudicial to the efficiency of the service; for while it tends to deteriorate the spirit of the regulars by depriving them of the first chance of meeting the enemy, it exposes the others to the influence of bribery, which constitutes so prominent a feature of Oriental warfare. Omer Pacha well understands the disadvantages resulting therefrom, and will soon have established a more healthy system. Already he has succeeded in inspiring the troops with a degree of self-confidence, quite unprecedented, by merely avoiding that error into which Turkish Generals so often fall, of detaching small bodies of troops, who are cut up by the enemy without object and without result. Individually, he is perhaps somewhat destitute of the élan which is generally associated with the character of a Guerilla chief, and yet without detracting from his character as a master in the art of modern war, there is no species of campaigning which he understands so well as that which he has successfully waged in Montenegro and the other hill countries of the Turkish empire. Energy and caution are the two qualities indispensable to success in these countries, and these he possesses to an eminent degree. It may be deemed presumptuous in me to pass an opinion upon one whose fame is world-wide; but that very fact must be my excuse, that those who are entitled to universal admiration are likewise subject to universal criticism. I have heard it urged that Fuad Pacha, the present Grand Vizier, who displayed much ability in the conduct of the war against the rebels in Thessalyand Epirus in 1854, would have succeeded better in the present hostilities. But, on the other hand, if the Grand Vizier be gifted with a greater amount of dash, Omer Pacha possesses a cooler judgement and a larger experience than any man in the Turkish empire; and before leaving the subject, I would call attention to the meritorious service which he has rendered to the Sultan under all circumstances. Disgraced without cause, he has faithfully adhered to the country of his adoption, displaying through good report and evil report an integrity which does honour to his principles. For, be it remembered, that he is bound by no ties of blood or nationality, and that treachery to Turkey would probably serve as a passport to the highest honours in Austria or Russia.

Apologising for this digression, I would now return to Osman Pacha and the column whom I have left so far to the rear. Late in the afternoon we arrived at Krustach, a position somewhat similar to Koryta, and of equal importance as regards the military occupation of the country. The valley is at this point shut in on either hand by hills of just sufficient height to give an advantageous command to a defending force; these are connected by a cross range, that present an apparently impassable barrier to an advancing foe. This position is surmounted by a small fort with a court-yard, whose walls are pierced for musketry. Four guns of indifferent quality are here mounted, commanding the approaches on either side, while three guard-houses, each capable of holding two or three companies, have been built on the most elevated positions, flanking the approach from the NW. The garrison consisted of two battalions commanded by a Wallack colonel, who might have passed but for his fez for an officer in the Russian service, so much did he resemble one of that nation in physiognomy. He appeared to be an active and intelligent officer, and had, I heard, rendered good service during the Eastern war. The appearance of the valley that night was strange and picturesque. Hundreds of fires stretched far up the sides of the cradle of hills in which our bivouac was formed, while a regular line of light marked the chain of outposts which crowned the surrounding heights. Head-quarters might be recognised by a large paper lantern suspended on a high stick close to the camp-fire, around which lay Osman Pacha, one of his staff, the Affghan Dervish, and myself, all sleeping quite as comfortably as though we had never known a bed. Trumpets sounded at 5 A.M. for a start; and, having ascended to the fort, we found the sun struggling for the mastery with the clouds on the tops of the adjacent hills. The army was now in full motion; the regular infantry defiled in something like order down the narrow path, which had been imperceptible to us on the preceding evening. The Bashi Bazouks, on the other hand, might be seen streaming down the hill-side, jumping, rolling, and tumbling in strange confusion. Having inspected the fort we joined in with these, and rode down a descent, which would have been impracticable for any save the sure-footed iron-plated horses of the East. After traversing the valley for some miles, the rugged line of Piwa closed in upon us on the left, and a black impenetrable mountain seemed to bar our farther progress. After three quarters of an hour's ascent we were glad to halt. Clambering to a grassy knoll, we made a frugal meal of the hardest of biscuit soaked in muddy water, the only food, by the way, which the troops tasted from the time of leaving Gasko until their return. These biscuits are manufactured at Constantinople, and are so hard as to be uneatable unless soaked; they, however, form a good substitute for bread, which is seldom to be procured. But we must not linger too long, for already the sun is high in the heavens. On, on, once more, brave little horses and unflinching men; your labours will soon be rewarded: and thus they toiled on, until, with sobbing flanks and perspiring brows, the highest requisite point was reached. Stretching away to our right front was a grassy glade, looking like velvet after the stony wilderness we had just left: a pine wood on the left gave it all the appearance of an English park, which was only dispelled by the extraordinary sight which now met the eye. Behind a dip in the ground were collected a considerable body of irregular horse and foot, who were awaiting our approach in all the magnificence of banners, kettledrums, sackbuts, psalteries, and all kinds of possible and impossible instruments of music. No sooner did we approach than away they went, horse and foot, shouting and blowing and waving their flags. The idea seemed contagious, for it was instantaneously followed by Osman Pacha and everyone who bestrode any kind of beast, prominent amongst whom the Affghan might be seen, flourishing his lance well to the fore. The glade opened out into a valley of inconsiderable size, which has witnessed more than one encounter between the Christians and Turks. Only the previous winter an engagement took place, in which the Turks, notwithstanding that they remained masters of the position, had from forty to fifty men put hors de combat. The timber here was of far finer growth than any I had yet seen, and the numerous oaks and elms lying with uptorn roots betokened the violence of the storms which rage. Many of them were lying midway across our line of march, and it was found necessary to remove them to admit of a free passage. This was soon effected, though perhaps with a little more noise than is consistent with English ideas of order. We had by this time entered the Pass of Dugah, formed by the extremities of Piwa on the left, and Banian on the right. The slopes on either hand are wooded, that of Banian to much the greatest extent. It is some fifteen miles in length, and consists of a series of open spaces, connected by narrow defiles, whose bottoms resemble the bed of a dry stream. The scenery is generally pretty, and abounds with interest from its being a constant bone of contention between the rival factions. As a defensive position it is undoubtedly strong; but there is nothing in the nature of the ground in reality to impede the advance of a determined force. While halted in one of the open spaces which I have mentioned, we discovered a hole or cavern in the side of the hill, capable of holding at least two hundred men. Doubtless this is a constant resort of the freebooters and other lawless ruffians who infest this part of the country. It was here that the European Consuls were nearly meeting their deaths, although accompanied by the Secretary of the Montenegrin Prince, when employed in making arrangements for the relief of Niksich, which was then invested.

It was dark before we reached the extremity of the valley, and little did we then think under what circumstances we should next see it. The latter portion of our march lay through a wood of hazel and other small trees, intersected here and there by pathways. Here we were met by more irregulars, and, debouching from the high land, we found a portion of the garrison of Niksich drawn up on the opposite bank of a little stream which flowed beneath us. The contour of the surrounding country is very remarkable: the gray heights of Piwa behind us, Drobniak to our left, and Banian looking green by comparison on the right, while the rocky mountains of Karatag form a dark and gloomy foreground to the picture.

During the ensuing night the rain descended in torrents, rendering the spongy ground on which we had bivouacked very much the reverse of a desirable resting-place. In vain I waited for an improvement in the weather, which only became worse and worse; and eventually I started in pursuit of that portion of the troops which had left at early dawn in charge of the provisions for Niksich. These consisted of 65,000 okes of meal and biscuit, with a few head of horned cattle. The last commodity appeared to me to be scarcely necessary, as we met some hundreds of bullocks being driven out to graze in the valley, while the presence of our force rendered such a measure safe. How these were generally supplied with forage I am at a loss to conjecture, since the Mussulman population were unable to venture more than one mile from the town, except in bodies of 500 armed men. The distance to the town from the commencement of the valley is about six miles, through a broad and well-watered pasture land. In parts this has been ploughed and devoted to the produce of grain, burnt stubble of which denoted the destructive ferocity of the neighbouring Montenegrins. The new line of frontier recently defined by the European Commission scarcely tends to promote a pacific adjustment of existing difficulties. On the contrary, the line of demarcation as it now is must inevitably lead to further complications. Situated at the apex of a triangle, the town and plain of Niksich offer a tempting bait to the lawless brigands, who infest the mountains which form two of its sides, and who keep the unfortunate Mussulman population in terror of their lives. At the south-eastern extremity of the plain stands the town of Niksich, a small, dirty, and irregular collection of buildings, all huddled together in the closest possible vicinity to the ruined fort, as though seeking the protection of its mouldering walls. Of the origin of the fort I could learn little, save from an inscription over the arched entrance, from which it appears to have been built by the son of an old and influential Albanian chieftain about 200 years ago. Two square towers, containing five pieces of ordnance, form the principal feature in the defensive works; but the whole place is in so ricketty a condition that, were a cannonade to be opened from its walls, they would inevitably come down about the ears of their defenders. From the easternmost of these towers the town runs out some few hundred yards towards the Montenegrin frontier; but all egress upon that side is out of the question, as there is ever a bullet in readiness for anyone who may be so rash as to cross a certain green patch of grass, which appears to be accepted as the legitimate boundary of the two provinces, although not precisely specified as such. At this point the Turkish sentries are withdrawn, but farther to the south a small white building serves as a guard-house, whence sentries are supplied to form a cordon round that portion of the frontier. On arriving at Niksich, we--that is, Osman Pacha's principal staff officer and myself--paid a visit to the Mudir, whom we found sitting in dignified conclave with his whole Medjlis. The Mudir, a magnificent Albanian, standing about six feet four inches, and of proportionate girth, welcomed us most cordially, and appeared a person of far greater intelligence than most of his class. He bitterly lamented the increase of suffering, resulting from the change in the line of frontier. 'Attacks by the Montenegrins and their friends,' said he, 'are now of daily occurrence, and there seems to be no chance of any improvement in our condition.' He expressed great confidence, however, in the advantages to be derived from Omer Pacha's arrival, and took a clear and sound view of things generally. He argued, correctly enough, that the rebels would stand a good chance of being literally starved into submission during the ensuing winter and spring, since the occupation of the country by the Turkish troops had prevented them from getting in their harvest, while the benighted frenzy which they had themselves displayed in the wanton destruction of the crops had deterred the neighbouring landowners from cultivating their fields. But the open intelligent face of our friend, the Mudir, lit up, more especially when telling us of some of the dours which he had made against the rebels; and in good sooth he looked better fitted for such employment, judging from his great length and breadth, than for sitting hour after hour on his haunches, emitting clouds of tobacco-smoke, and reflecting upon the individuality of God, and the plurality of wives, reserved in the next world for all those who say their prayers regularly, and kill a sufficient number of Feringhees in this. These stereotyped notions, however, regarding the tenets of Mahometanism are fast losing credence, just in proportion as the growth of European ideas is undermining its very foundation. I do not say that Mussulmans are becoming more religious or more elevated from their contact with Christian peoples. Indeed, I rather incline to the opposite opinion; but the European tendencies which prevail are marked clearly enough by the facile adroitness with which the followers of the Prophet contrive to evade the injunctions of the Koran, whether it be in the matter of wines and strong drinks, or the more constitutional difficulty touching loans, debts, and the like. For myself, I rather incline to the view of the old Pacha, who, after listening with his habitual patience to the long-winded arguments of a Protestant missionary, completely dumb-foundered that excellent divine by remarking that he (the Pacha) felt quite convinced of the similarity of their creeds, since the only apparent difference was, that the Christian has three Gods and one wife, while the Mussulman has three wives and one God. Even in this last matter, the plurality of wives, a marvellous amendment is visible. It is probably owing to the expense attendant thereon, and also to the little fact, that it is not quite in accordance with the spirit of the age to drown, or otherwise destroy, those women who indulge their very pardonable and womanly frailty of wrangling and fighting one with another. But, granting all this, it is impossible not to perceive that the position of Turkish women is daily improving. All of a certain class receive some education; and I never yet spoke to any intelligent Turk on the subject without hearing him deplore the existence of those laws in the Koran which would deprive the world of that which renders it most enjoyable. That the time will come when the religious influences of Mahometanism will cease to offer a bar to all progress and advancement, is sufficiently evident, and it consequently behoves Europe to guard against the re-establishment of moral heathenism on the ruin of fanatical Islamism.

Returning to the council-chamber of the Mudir of Niksich, I would call attention to the similarity of expression and venerable appearance of nearly every member of the Medjlis. This is one of the faults of the system, that an undue preponderance is thereby given to the ideas of a certain class.

From the experience of those Europeans who have had good opportunities of forming an opinion, it would seem that this double government of Pacha and Medjlis works badly, owing to the ignorance and want of capacity of those from whom the latter are selected. It would, therefore, be far more salutary were they only permitted to advise in place of having a vote; absolute authority being vested in the Pacha, who should be held personally responsible that the rights of the people be not infringed, and rigorously punished if convicted of malpractices.

Many will doubtless deny the advantages to be thus derived; but it is self-evident that in half-civilised countries power should be in the hands of as few as possible.

It is not my intention to enter the lists as the champion of the Ottoman Government, whose apathy and insincerity cannot be too strongly condemned; but I contend that governments, like everything else, must be judged by comparison, and that the only true measure of the merits of a government is the moral and social condition of the people whom it rules. The Turkish Government, whether regarded in its central or provincial bearings, is decidedly in advance of its subjects. In its diplomatic relations, in monetary and financial schemes, Turkey has at any rate acquired a certain amount of credit, while an increase of the revenue from four to nearly twelve millions within the past thirty years, and the continued increase of the Christian population, is a certain proof of the diminution of oppression, and proves conclusively that a remnant of vitality still exists in her veins.

[Footnote Q: The British member of the European Commission for defining the frontier of Montenegro.]

## CHAPTER XIV.

Return to Gasko--Thunderstorm--Attacked by Rebels--Enemy repulsed--Retrograde Movement--Eventful Night--Turkish Soldiers murdered--Montenegrin Envoy--Coal-Pit--Entrenched Camp assaulted--Return of Omer Pacha to Mostar--Distinctive Character of Mahometan Religion--Naval Reorganisation--Military Uniforms--Return to Mostar--Dervisch Bey--Zaloum--Express Courier--Giovanni--Nevresign--Fortified Barrack--Mostar--Magazine--Barracks--Wooden Blockhouses--European Commission--Tour of the Grand Vizier--Enquiry into Christian Grievances--Real Causes of Complaint--Forcible Abduction of Christian Girls--Prince Gortschakoff's Charges--The Meredits--Instincts of Race.

On our return from the town we found the leading battalions in the act of crossing the stream which separates the valley from the overhanging woodland. The 900 ponies, now deprived of their burden, carried in lieu thereof sick soldiers from Niksich, or such as preferred riding to walking. Little order prevailed, and it is only wonderful that the consequences of entering a defile more than an hour after midday should not have proved more disastrous than they actually did. In vain I added my remonstrances to those of some of the staff, who were intelligent enough to predict evil. The order had been issued. The advance guard had already marched, and it was too late to countermand the departure. Thus saying, Osman

Pacha crossed the stream and ascended to the high ground, now covered with a confused mass of bipeds and quadrupeds. At this moment the rain, which had ceased during the past hour, began to descend once more in torrents, accompanied by vivid flashes of lightning and thunder, which, though still distant, reverberated through the woods with grand effect. In the midst of this we retraced our steps until about 4 P.M., when the centre of the column, with the baggage and head-quarters, defiled from the woods into one of the open spaces, of which mention has been made. The General informed me of his intention to halt there until the morning; and he could not have found a spot better calculated for the purpose, since, by massing the troops in the centre, they would have been out of range of the surrounding heights, and a double line of sentries would have been the only precaution absolutely necessary. For some reason he, however, subsequently changed his mind, and the delay which had taken place only made matters worse. The advance guard of four battalions, under Yaya Pacha, had continued the march in ignorance of the halt of the main body, and were ere this out of hearing or chance of recall. Scarcely had we recommenced our advance when a dropping shot in the rear gave us the first announcement that the enemy had taken advantage of our false step, and was bent on harassing what would now assume the appearance of a retreat.

The shots, which were at first few and distant, soon increased, and by the time that the Affghan and myself had reached the rear of the column the action appeared to have become general. Ali Pacha, who commanded the rear-guard, now committed the grave error of halting the three battalions of his brigade, and wasted most valuable time in performing desultory movements, and in firing volleys of grape and musketry, without arriving at any practical results. At one point, however, the rebels, who were advancing in force with loud cries of fanatical vengeance, received a substantial check. Two companies of Turks had been concealed on either side of the defile, which was narrow at this point. Concealment was facilitated by approaching darkness, and it was only at a given signal that they rose and poured a deadly volley into the ranks of the advancing foe, who immediately fell back. This circumstance appeared to damp their ardour, and they contented themselves with running in small parties along the flank of our line of march; two or three would dash down the sloping banks, and, having discharged their pieces without aim or precision, would return to the safety afforded by the rocks and trees. It was between 6 and 7 o'clock before the order to resume the march was issued. And now began a scene which none who witnessed are likely to forget to their dying day: deeply tragical it might have been, but fortunately circumstances combined to render it merely ridiculous, as reflected in the mirror of memory. The rain still fell heavily, lying in places to the depth of nearly a foot, and converting all the ground that was not rocky into a slippery quagmire. So profound was the darkness, that it was literally impossible to see any object six inches from one's eyes, and it was only by the occasional flashes from the firelocks of the persevering enemy and the forked lightning that we could realise the surrounding scene. By the light of the last were revealed horses and men falling in all directions, and I may safely say, that some of the 'crumplers' received that night would have shaken the nerve of the hardest steeplechase rider. For my own part I preferred walking, after my horse had fallen twice, and with this object proceeded to dismount, but on bringing my leg to the ground, as I imagined, I made a rapid descent of about eight feet. On clambering up I was met with a sharp blow on the face from what I believe to have been the butt of a Turkish musket, and my horse was not to be found. About half an hour later, while feeling for the road, to my great satisfaction, I placed my hand upon my English saddle, and thus repossessed myself of my steed. No need to dilate farther on the events of that disastrous evening. Suffice to say that, after some hours more of scrambling and toiling, falling frequently over the stones and trees which were strewn plentifully across the path, we reached the spot where the advanced body had arrived some four hours previously, and had succeeded, in spite of the rain, in kindling a few fires. It was close upon midnight when Ali Pacha arrived at head-quarters to report that the rear-guard had reached the bivouac, though nothing was known as to the losses incurred in men, horses, or provisions. All that was certain was that one gun had been abandoned, the mule which carried it having rolled down a ravine. This was never found, as the rebels, who passed the night within ten minutes' walk of our bivouac, had carried it off before the arrival of the force sent back at daybreak to effect its recovery. Our loss, however, proved to be insignificant--two killed and six wounded, and a few ponies, &c., missing. As might be supposed, the Slavish newspapers magnified the affair into a great and decisive victory for the rebels. It is true that it reflected little credit on Osman Pacha; and it might have been fully as disastrous to the Turks as their worst enemies could have desired, had not the intense darkness of the night, the heavy rain, and the want of pluck in the Christians (a fault of which they cannot in general be accused), combined to get them out of the scrape without any serious loss. The two whose deaths it was impossible to disallow, as their mangled bodies gave evidence thereof, were foully butchered by these long-suffering Christians. It came about as follows:--An officer and three soldiers had remained a little in rear of the column, being footsore with the march. As the rebels came swiftly and quietly along, one of the soldiers, believing them to be a Turkish regiment, made some observation. In a moment he and his comrade were seized, and, while receiving many assurances of safety, were stripped to the skin. The officer and the third soldier instantly concealed themselves behind some of the projecting rocks, within ten yards of the spot, and thus became auditors of the ensuing tragedy. No sooner had the rebels stripped their unfortunate captives, than they fell upon them en masse, literally making pin-cushions of their naked bodies. Throughout that long and painful night did those two men lie hid in jeopardy of their lives, and glad must they have been when they saw the rebels retracing their blood-stained steps on the following morning, and more grateful still when the arrival of the Turkish force enabled them to feel assured of life and liberty. The following afternoon we returned to Krustach, where we found a Montenegrin emissary, who was journeying homeward, having had an interview with Omer Pacha. He was a finely built and handsome man, dressed in his national costume, with a gold-braided jacket, and decorated with a Russian medal and cross, for his services against Turkey at a time when Russia was at peace with that power. He had been Superintendent of the Montenegrin workmen at Constantinople, and had consequently seen something of European manners, although unacquainted with any language save Slave and some Turkish. He told me that he had left 400 followers in Piwa; but this I found did not exactly coincide with a statement he had made to Omer Pacha, and it subsequently transpired that his body guard amounted to about double that number. This worthy asked me to accompany him to Cettigne, but circumstances conspired to prevent my accepting the invitation; and so we separated, he to Cettigne, we to Gasko on the following day.

During one of the halts on the line of march, I found the mouth of what must have been a coal-pit of large dimensions. The entrance of this was on the bank of a dry stream, and several masses of what appeared to be a concrete of lignite and coal betokened the existence of the latter in a purer form within the bowels of the surrounding country. This I showed to Omer Pacha, who said that he would adopt my suggestion of having it worked by military labour for the purpose of consumption during the winter months. In several places, I subsequently came across the same characteristics, which convince me of the existence of a spurious description of coal in large quantities in the province. In Bosnia it is plentiful, and of a very superior quality.

Some miles before we reached the camp we were met by Omer Pacha and his staff combat. Omer's face wore a grave expression when we met, and his 'Eh bien, Monsieur, nous avons perdu un canon sans utilité' boded ill for the peace of Osman Pacha. It was a pleasing duty to be able to refute the assertion that this last had lost his head on the occasion in question. Although guilty of grievous error of judgement, the other more pitiful charge could hardly be laid to his account, since he never for a moment lost his habitual sangfroid and self-possession.

The subsequent operations during 1861 were scarcely of a more decisive nature than those in the early part of the campaign. They consisted for the most part of slight skirmishes, which, though unimportant in themselves, tended to establish the Turks in their occupation of the country, and produced a good moral effect.

One event, however, deserves notice, as giving fair evidence of the respective merits of the belligerent parties. In pursuance of the plan which he had originally devised, Omer Pacha established a permanent fortified camp in Piwa. Twelve battalions under Dervisch Pacha were concentrated at this point; and at the time of the contest which I am about to describe, Omer Pacha was himself present. Reduced to the greatest straits by famine and the presence of the Turkish troops, and inspired doubtless by the knowledge of the Generalissimo's presence in the camp, the rebels resolved to make a desperate onslaught upon the entrenchments.

On the morning of October 26, a strong force was despatched from camp to procure forage, wood, and other necessaries. While thus employed, the enemy, favoured by the formation of the surrounding country, made a sudden and well-sustained attack upon this force, in conjunction with a consentaneous assault upon the entrenchments. With more judgement than is generally found amongst Turkish commanders, the foraging party was brought back to camp, though not before it had suffered a considerable loss. In the meantime charge upon charge was being made by the half-naked savages who formed the Christian army, against the enclosed space which was dignified by the name of an entrenched camp. Three times they forced an entrance, and three times were they driven out at the point of the bayonet, while the guns mounted on the works made wide gaps in their retreating columns. After several hours' hard fighting, in which both sides displayed exemplary courage, the assailants were compelled to withdraw, leaving many hundred dead upon the field. The Turkish loss was something under a hundred, owing to the advantage they derived from fighting under the cover of their guns and walls.

Shortly after this event Omer Pacha returned to Mostar, contenting himself with holding the various passes and other points on the frontier, which enabled him to keep an unremitting watch over the disturbed district.

Early in the spring of 1862 he returned to the frontier, which he will doubtless pacify before the extreme heat and drought shall have forced him to suspend military operations. With this view eighteen battalions of infantry and 3,000 irregulars have been concentrated at and about Trebigné, which he has this year made his base of operations. The judicious disposal of his troops, which he has effected, have driven Luca Vukalovitch and his band of hornets to take refuge in Suttorina, adjacent to the Austrian territory. This circumstance caused the Austrians at the end of last year to enter that district for the purpose of destroying certain batteries, which were considered to be too close to the Austrian frontier. The legality of this measure is doubtful; yet it may be believed that the step was not taken with any view to promoting hostilities with Turkey.

The final success of the Turkish arms can scarcely be long delayed, since starvation must inevitably effect all in which the sword may fail. The armed occupation of the country during the past year has at any rate so far worked good, that it has effectually prevented the rebellious Christians from getting in the crops which belonged to themselves or their weaker neighbours, while it has enabled such of the Mussulmans as chose to do so to reap their harvest in security. Should these expectations, however, not be realised, the result would indeed be serious to the Ottoman empire. In such case either her already rotten exchequer must receive its death-blow, or she will be compelled to evacuate the Herzegovina, a course which would be gladly welcomed by her enemies, since it would probably be but the first step towards the dismemberment of the whole empire.

Before quitting the army, I would fain pay a passing tribute to the good qualities of the Turkish soldiers. Having seen them under circumstances of no ordinary difficulty and privations, I found them ever cheerful and contented with their unenviable lot. Uninfluenced by feelings of patriotism--for such a word exists not in their language--unaffected by the love of glory, which they have not sufficient education to comprehend, the only motives by which they are actuated are their veneration for their Sultan and the distinctive character of their religion. It would be well for their Sultan did he appreciate the sterling military qualities of his people. With good management and honest reform, an army might be created which, if inferior in matériel to those of certain European powers, would in the matter of personnel be sufficiently good to render the Turkish dominions perfectly secure from hostile invasion, which is now very far from the case. At present, unfortunately, his whole attention is devoted to the manning and equipment of the navy, for the amelioration of which large sums of money are paid and heavy debts incurred. The visionary character of his ambitious projects on this head is apparent to all but himself, since the Turkish navy can scarcely be expected ever to attain more than a fifth or sixth-rate excellence. The recent changes in the dress of the army betoken that some attention has been devoted of late to the subject. Nothing can be more desirable than an assimilation of the uniform to the natural style of costume; and the loose Zouave dresses of the army of the Turkish imperial guard[R] are not only better adapted to soldiers who do not indulge in the luxury of beds and the like, than the tight-fitting garments heretofore in use, but present a far more workmanlike appearance, for the simple reason that they understand better how to put them on.

After a month's sojourn in the tents of the Osmanlis, the rapid shortening of the days warned me of the necessity for pushing on if I wished to see the more peaceable portion of the country, before the snows of winter should render travelling impossible. Already the day had arrived when the first fall of snow had taken place in the previous year.

Despite the hardships indispensable from the kind of life we had been living, it was with much regret that I bade farewell to my hospitable entertainers, and started once more on my solitary rambles. For the first day, at least, I was destined to have company, as the Pacha of Bosnia's private Secretary was about to return to Bosna Serai, having fulfilled a mission on which he had been sent to the camp of the Commander-in-Chief. My object was to return to Mostar by way of Nevresign, which, as well as being new ground to me, forms a portion of the projected line of defence. After waiting no less than five hours and a half for an escort of Bashi Bazouks, who, with true Turkish ideas of the value of time, presented themselves at 12.30, having been warned to be in attendance at 7 A.M., we at length got under weigh. These irregulars were commanded by Dervisch Bey, one of the principal Beys in that neighbourhood. Some twenty years ago his father, a devout Mussulman, and a cordial hater of Christians, whom, it must be acknowledged, he lost no opportunity of oppressing, built for himself a large square house flanked with towers, and otherwise adapted for defensive purposes. This is situated about six miles from Gasko, and here he lived in considerable affluence. Taken one day at an unguarded moment, he was murdered by the Christians, and his mantle descended upon his son, who, if he has not the same power or inclination to oppress, shows himself perfectly ready to do battle on all occasions against the murderers of his father. This individual, then, mounted on a good useful-looking horse, and loaded with silver-hilted daggers, pistols, and other weapons of offence, was destined to be our guide. Our road lay through a long narrow defile, which, like most parts of the Herzegovina, abounds with positions capable of defence. After five hours' travelling we arrived at Zaloum, a small military station situated at the highest point of the pass. I did not see any attempt at fortifications; but, as all the villages are built quite as much with a view to defence as convenience, these are hardly necessary. Every house is surrounded by a court-yard, in most cases loopholed. Taking up our quarters at the only house capable of affording the most ordinary shelter, we passed the evening, as far as I was concerned, pleasantly enough. The Secretary, a middle-aged and very affable Slave, was also somewhat of a bon vivant, and, with the help of sundry adjuncts which he carried with him, we made a very good meal. The habit of drinking rakee, eating cheese, and other provocatives of thirst before dining, is quite as rife in these parts of the empire as at Stamboul, and it frequently happens that the dinner-hour of a fashionable man is later than in London during the height of the season. Breakfasting at twelve, they do not touch food again till dinner-time, and even then their repeated nips of rakee taken in the hour previous to the repast renders them little disposed for eating. Shortly after we had commenced dinner at Zaloum, a great chattering and confusion in the court-yard proclaimed a new arrival. This proved to be Asiz Bey, an aide-de-camp of Omer Pacha, who was on his road to Mostar. Snatching a hurried meal, he once more mounted, and pushed on in the darkness, with the intention of not pulling rein again until his arrival in Mostar. Later in the evening an excited agriculturist made his appearance, and with much humility demanded the return of his pack-saddle, which he affirmed that one of my servants had stolen. It fell out in this wise: I had engaged a certain youth of the Greek faith, named Giovanni, to look after my baggage-ponies, which he invariably allowed to stray whenever most required. On the occasion of our leaving Gasko one of these was, as usual, absent without leave, and on his being discovered, the pack-saddle in which these long-suffering animals pass their existence had been removed. Giovanni, whose pilfering habits were only equalled by his disregard of truth, replaced the missing article in the simplest way, by doing unto others as they had done unto him, and appropriated the first saddle he came across. To allow the saddle to return to Gasko was impossible, as I could not have proceeded on my journey without it; so I induced the owner to part with it at a considerable profit, mulcting Giovanni of the same. The following morning we descended into the plain of Nevresign, one of the seven or eight large plains in the province.

The road approaching the town passes between two cemeteries--that of the Mussulmans on the right being the most pleasantly situated, for thus it was that, even in death, they were more regarded than their less-favoured Christian brethren. On the outskirts I noticed a very primitive movable house, strongly characteristic of the kind of life led by the people: it consisted of two skates, with a hurdle laid across for flooring and others for walls, the whole being thatched. In this the shepherd sleeps when he pens his cattle: this he does in a very small space, shifting his position every night, and thus practically manuring the country. The town itself has little worthy of notice, save the new fortified barrack which the Turks are constructing. No labourers were, however, engaged upon it at the time of my visit: it consists of an oblong work, with bastions at the angles, on each of which it is intended to mount three guns. It was proposed to build accommodation for 1,600 men, but the size of the work did not appear to me to warrant the belief that it would hold so many. There will be no necessity for the townspeople to take shelter within its walls in the event of an attack, as it immediately overhangs the town, and is itself commanded by the hills in its rear. The engineer officer who conducted me over it informed me that an earthwork would be thrown up on the most commanding position, and two block-houses built at other points. The arrangements for obtaining a supply of water appeared simple; and as it is the only attempt at modern fortification which I have seen in Turkey, I shall be curious to hear of its completion.

Leaving Nevresign one crosses two mountains, which, with the exception of about an hour and a half distance, are traversed by a road. Save one in course of construction from Mostar to Metcovich, it is the only attempt at road-making in the province. It is bad enough, as all Turkish roads are, their engineers having not the slightest idea of levelling. They take the country as they find it, apparently thinking that a zigzag, no matter at what slope the angles may be, is the highest triumph of their art. Until our arrival at Blagai, six miles from Mostar, an escort was deemed necessary, though it was really of not the slightest use, since the rebels, if so inclined, might have disposed of the whole party without once showing themselves. On nearing Mostar I looked with curiosity for any signs of progress in the new powder magazine or barracks, which are situated in the plain outside the town. They both appeared in precisely the same condition as when I left, save for the absence of some hundreds of ponies, which were at that moment eating mouldy hay at Gasko and its vicinity. In the barrack square several block-houses which Omer Pacha had ordered appeared to be in a state of completion. These are made of wood and have two stories, each house being capable of containing about two companies of infantry. The walls are loopholed and of sufficient thickness to resist musket balls: the use to which they were to be applied was the protection of working parties and small detachments during the construction of more permanent defences; and as the rebels are without carcases or liquid fire-balls or other scientific implements of destruction, it is possible that they may answer their purpose well enough.

At the British Consulate I found Mr. H., the Consul at Bosna Serai, who was on his road to Ragusa, where the European Commission for carrying out reforms in

Turkey was about to reassemble, with the view of watching the progress of events. Little good could be expected to result from their deliberations, for matters had not been in any way simplified since their adjournment two months before. The sincerity of the individual members of the Commission cannot be called in question; but what avails that, when other agents of the governments so represented apply themselves with assiduity to stultify the very measures which their colleagues are endeavouring to effect. As might have been anticipated, their sittings at Ragusa proved as ineffectual as those at Mostar, and in three weeks' time they once more adjourned, and have not since reassembled. Whatever difference of opinion may have existed amongst the members on this point, at any rate they professedly agreed that it is for the interest of these provinces that the Turkish rule should remain inviolate, but that this rule must be very decidedly ameliorated. Of its sincerity in wishing to bring this about the Porte will find it difficult to convince the Christian malcontents, so deeply rooted is their mistrust. Secret agents are not wanting to check any spirit of wavering which may show itself in the insurgents. In the meanwhile both Bosnia and Herzegovina are being rapidly exhausted. Even in peaceable times, the people of the Herzegovina had to draw their supplies of grain from Bosnia, while the import trade of both provinces more than doubled the export in value. The demand for horses for military purposes has of late still farther crippled commercial enterprise, as the people are thereby deprived of the only means of transport in the country. At Mostar, even, it was impossible to buy coals, as the peasants were afraid of exposing their horses to the probability of being pressed, with the certainty of remaining unpaid.

The foregoing remarks may appear to corroborate ill my oft-repeated assertion of the immunity of the Christians from persecution by the constituted Mussulman authorities. A distinction should be made between oppression and misgovernment, the existence of which last is fully admitted on all hands. It applies in an almost equal degree to the professors of all religions in Turkey; and when the Christians have been induced by designing minds, as has sometimes been the case, to pour out to the world a torrent of grievances, these have been proved in almost all instances to have been as much imaginary as real; such at least was the opinion of the Grand Vizier, after his visit of enquiry through European Turkey in 1860; and his views, which might otherwise be deemed prejudiced, were supported by Mr. L----, the Consul-General at Belgrade, who was deputed by the British Ambassador to attend the Ottoman functionary. That gentleman's opinion--concurred in, as it is, by almost all British officials--is especially worthy of attention, since the greater part of his life has been passed in the Turkish dominions, and a large share of his attention devoted to this particular subject. At Widdin, a petition was presented, signed by 300 persons, complaining of the local authorities. These names were mostly forgeries, and even the alleged grievances were of a trivial nature; outrages, and forced conversion to Islamism, could nowhere be proved. The source whence the petition emanated may be shrewdly guessed, since M. Sokoloff, the Russian Consul at Widdin, was removed to Jerusalem only a few days before the commencement of the enquiry. One subject of complaint was the appointment of the bishops by the patriarch at Constantinople, which strongly confirms the supposition of its Russian origin. The petition was moreover presented by one Tuno, a Rayah, who had been turned out of the Medjlis for corruption, and was at the time a hanger-on at the Russian consulate. Those few who acknowledged to having signed the document, stated that they believed it to have been a remonstrance against the pig tax.

The second ground of complaint was that the Cadi had interfered in the affairs of the Christians; i.e. in matters of inheritance, and in the administration of the property of minors. This also proved untenable, although, in the course of the enquiry, it transpired that something of the sort had occurred at Crete, which was ingeniously perverted to suit their purpose on the occasion in question.

Thirdly, it was alleged that the Christian members of the Medjlis were allowed no voice in its deliberations. This the Bishop even denied. Had they said that their opinions were of little weight, it would have been nearer the truth. Nor can we wonder at this, since it is in vain that we look for any spirit of independence among the Christian members; and this not more in consequence of the domineering spirit of the Turks, than from the natural disposition of the Christians, which is cringing and corrupt. Time and education can alone effect a change for the better. The government may, by the promulgation of useful edicts, and by the establishment of schools common to all religions, materially hasten this desirable end; but in the present condition of the Christian population, it is questionable whether more harm than good would not result from the proclamation of social equality.

The veritable grounds of complaint, on which the petition in question did not touch, it is within the power of the government to remove; and this, we may confidently anticipate, will be done.

Equality before the law is the principal and first thing to be established, and such at present is not the case. Christian evidence, for example, is received in criminal, but not in civil causes, i.e. in questions concerning property. Moreover, even in criminal causes of any importance, the decision of the inferior courts, where Christian evidence is admissible, is referred for confirmation to superior courts, where such testimony is not accepted. In defence of this it is urged, that Turkish property would be endangered, if, in the present demoralised state of society, Christian evidence were admitted. But, while advancing this argument, it is forgotten that this state is traceable to the lax and vicious system pursued in the Mussulman courts, where, as the only way of securing justice for the Christians, Mussulman witnesses are allowed to give false evidence.

Another abuse, of which the most is made by the enemies of Turkey, is the forcible abduction of Christian girls by Mussulmans. The practice has, however, almost died out, except in northern Albania; and yet it is this alone which formed the groundwork of the most important of Prince Gortschakoff's charges, viz. the forced conversion of Christians to Islamism. It would, doubtless, fall into disuse in that part of the country, were the offence dealt with as an ordinary police affair; but the clumsy machinery of Turkish law, however sincere may be its object, has done little to diminish the evil. Many schemes have been devised for its prevention. One was to make the girl appear before the court which rejects Christian evidence, and declare herself a Christian or Mussulman. If she confessed her faith, she was returned to her friends, and the ravisher nominally punished; but, as they almost always declared themselves to be Mahomedans, the Christians complained that fear or other undue pressure had been put upon them. To obviate this, it was decided that the girl should be sequestered in the house of the Bishop for three days previous to her making her profession of faith. This has, however, been discontinued, as it produced much scandal; and the question remains undecided.

Instincts of race are far stronger in Turkey than is generally supposed. In Albania, where the Mussulmans are deemed more fanatical than elsewhere, these are more powerful than even the instincts of religion. Thus, while other Christians are looked down upon and treated with severity, the Miridits, who are of Albanian blood, are allowed to wear their arms, and admitted to equal privileges with their Mahomedan fellow-countrymen. In Bosnia, more than anywhere throughout the empire, the question has been one of feudal origin, that is to say, of a privileged and unprivileged class, analogous to that which now occupies the Russians; although in Bosnia the former class has been gradually losing importance, and sinking into a lower position.

To the demoralised condition of the Christians themselves, then, combined with Turkish misgovernment, resulting from their semi-civilisation, may the existing unsatisfactory state of affairs be attributed, and not to any systematic oppression. It is the want of this, which renders it difficult for the Porte, now that the central power has been strengthened at the expense of the local, to take any decided steps for improving the position of the Christians; all that it can do is to place all upon a footing of legal equality, to encourage education, and to promote everything which shall have for its object the developement of the natural resources of the country.

## CHAPTER XV.

Excursion to Blato--Radobolya--Roman Road--Lichnitza--Subterraneous Passage--Duck-shooting--Roman Tombs--Coins and Curiosities--Boona--Old Bridge--Mulberry Trees--Blagai--Source of Boona River--Kiosk--Castle--Plain of Mostar--Legends--Silver Ore--Mineral Products of Bosnia--Landslip--Marbles--Rapids--Valley of the Drechnitza.

The week following upon my return to Mostar was devoted to excursions to different spots in the vicinity of the town. In one instance the pleasure was enhanced by the anticipation of some duck-shooting; for, as the event will show, the expectation was never realised. Our destination was Blato, a plain about nine miles distant, which all maps represent as a lake, but which does not deserve the name, as it is only flooded during the winter months. The party consisted of M. Gyurcovich, the Hungarian dragoman of the British consulate; the Russian Consul; his domestic, a serf strongly addicted to the use of ardent drinks, of which he had evidently partaken largely on the occasion in question; a French doctor, who had many stories of the Spanish war, in which he had served; two other individuals, and myself.

About one hour from Mostar, we arrived at the source of the Radobolya, which flows through Mostar and falls into the Narenta near the old bridge. The road was sufficiently well defined, although needing repair in places. The walls on either side, as well as its general construction, proclaim its Roman origin. It was doubtless a part of the great main road from the east to Dalmatia. It is only at occasional points that it is so easily discernible, but sufficient evidence exists to show that on quitting the Albanian mountains it passed Stolatz, crossed the bridge at Mostar, and continued thence by a somewhat circuitous route to Spalatro. On emerging from the defile through which we had been marching, the plain of Blato lay extended before us, some nine or ten miles in length and four in breadth. The land, which must be extremely fertile, is cultivated in the spring, but only those cereals which are of the most rapid growth are produced; such as millet, Indian corn, and broom seed, from which a coarse description of bread is made. The Lichnitza, which runs through it, is a mere stream. It takes its rise near the Austro-Bosnian frontier, and loses itself in the hills which surround Blato. The plain is porous and full of holes, from which, in the late autumnal months, the waters bubble up. This continues until the river itself overflows, covering the entire plain to a considerable depth, in some parts as much as thirty-six feet. The original passage under the hills, by which the water escaped, is said to have been filled up at the time of the Turkish conquest. If such be true, it might be reopened with little cost and trouble, and the plain would thus be rendered most valuable to the province.

Arrived at the scene of operations, we lost little time in getting to work. A still evening, and a moon obscured by light clouds, promised well for sport; and we should doubtless have made a large bag had ordinary precautions been taken. These, however, were not deemed necessary by the majority of the party, who walked down in the open to the river's edge, smoking and chattering as though they expected the 'dilly-dills to come and be killed' merely for the asking. The result, I need not say, was our return almost empty-handed. Late in the evening we assembled round a large fire, to eat the dinner which our servants had already prepared; after which we courted sleep beneath the soothing influences of tales of love and war as related by our Æsculapian friend, who undeniably proved himself to have been a very Don Quixote. Early the following morning we were again afoot, and a few partridges, hares, and quail rewarded our exertions. Amongst the hills, where most of the game was shot, I noticed several old Roman tombs. Many of these were merely large shapeless blocks of stone, while others were of the proper sarcophagus form, ornamented with sculptures of considerable merit. On some were depicted men in armour, with shields and long straight swords, while others had two men with lances aimed at a deer between them. The absence of anything like moulding on the sides proves their great antiquity. In its place we find a rather graceful pattern, vines with leaves and grapes predominating; or, as in other cases, choruses of women holding hands and dancing. In no instance did I detect anything denoting immorality or low ideas, so prevalent in the sculptures of intermediate ages. Amongst these tombs, as also on the sites of the ancient towns, curiosities and coins are found. Of the last, small Hungarian silver pieces, and large Venetian gold pieces, are the most numerous; although Roman copper coins are by no means rare. Stones engraved with figures of Socrates and Minerva were shown to me, as having been found in the province, and it is only two years since, that two golden ear-rings of fifteen drachms weight, and about the size of pigeons' eggs, were dug up in the neighbourhood of Blato. About the same time a ring was found, of which the Pacha obtained possession. It was of iron, set with a stone only three tenths of an inch in diameter, on which were most beautifully engraved no fewer than nine figures of classical deities.

The ensuing day I devoted to a double expedition to Boona and Blagai. The former of these is about six miles distant, on the plain from Mostar. It consists of a few houses built by the rebellious Ali Pacha, who was Vizier at the time of Sir Gardner Wilkinson's visit to Herzegovina. That functionary's villa, which is now the country-house of the British Consul, is a moderate-sized yellow house, with little to recommend it save its situation at the confluence of the Boona and the Narenta. The former is spanned by a large bridge of fourteen arches, upon one of which is a Turkish inscription, from which it appears that it was repaired by the Turks in the year of the Hegira 1164--that is to say, 113 years ago.

The bridge is in all probability of Roman construction, though the Turkish habit of erasing all inscriptions, and substituting others in Turkish in their place, renders it impossible to fix precise dates. Near the villa stands a square house intended for the nurture of silk-worms, while a garden of 30,000 mulberry trees shows that Ali Pacha had pecuniary considerations in view as well as his domestic comfort. From Boona to Blagai is about six miles, and here also is a bridge of five arches across the Boona. Leaving the village, which stands on the banks of the river, we proceeded to its source. Pears, pomegranates, olives, and other fruit trees grow in great luxuriance, and two or three mills are worked by the rush of water, which is here considerable. The cavern from which the river pours in a dense volume, is about eight feet high, and situated at the foot of a precipitous cliff, under which stands a kiosk, the abode of our fighting friend the Affghan Dervish. Thence we proceeded to the castle, which stands on the summit of a craggy height, overlooking the village on the one side, and the road to Nevresign on the other. Speaking of this, Luccari says, 'Blagai stands on a rock above the river Bosna, fortified by the ancient Voivodas of the country to protect their treasure, as its name implies, Blagia (or Blago) signifying treasure.'[S]

It was governed by a Count, and the Counts of Blagai performed a distinguished part in the history of Herzegovina. Some of them, as the Boscenovich and the Hranich, are known for their misfortunes, having been compelled to seek refuge in Ragusa at the time of the Turkish invasion; and the last who governed 'the treasure city of Blagai' was Count George, who fled to the Ragusan territory in 1465.[T] The view to the southward over the plain country is extremely picturesque, but this portion of the battlements are completely ruined. On the north side they are in good preservation, and there wells exist, the cement of which looked as fresh as though it had been recently renovated.

In one of the batteries a brass gun was lying, of about 9lbs. calibre, with vent and muzzle uninjured. In the interior of the fort, shells of dwelling-houses, distributed angularly, denote the part of the building which was devoted to domestic purposes. In these the woodwork of the windows may still be seen, as well as stones projecting from the walls, on which the flooring of the upper stories must have rested. At the main entrance an oak case is rivetted into the wall to receive the beam, which barred the door. At the foot of the hill is a ruined church, in which some large shells of about thirteen inches diameter were strewed about. One of these was lying on the road side, as though it had been rolled from the castle above.

Having now seen all the lions of the neighbourhood, I bethought me of leaving Mostar once more, but this time with the intention of working northward. The ordinary route pursued by those whom business calls from Mostar to Bosna Serai is by Konitza, a village situated on the frontier, nearly due north of Mostar. To this course I at first inclined, but was induced to change my plans by the prospect of some chamois-hunting, in the valley of the Drechnitza. Having laid in a supply of bread and other necessaries, we, i.e. M. Gyurcovich and myself, made an early start, in hopes of reaching our destination on the same night.

Following the right bank of the Narenta, our course lay for a short time through the northernmost of the two plains at whose junction Mostar is situated. These, from the smooth and round appearance of the stones, with which their surface is strewed, lead to the supposition that this at one time was the bed of an important lake: this idea is confirmed by the legends of the country, which affirm the existence of rings in the sides of the mountains, to which it is rumoured that boats were moored of old. Whether this be true or not, the appearance of the place lends probability to the statement.

Shortly after leaving the town, there is a small square tower close to and commanding the river, which is here fordable. As we proceeded farther north it becomes rocky and narrow, and some small rapids occur at intervals. The bad state of the roads, and the ill condition of our baggage horses, rendered it necessary to halt several hours short of the point which we had intended to reach that night. Having, therefore, cleared out an outhouse devoted in general to looms, green tobacco, hens, cats, and the like, we made our arrangements for passing the night. While thus engaged a peasant brought me a tolerably large specimen of silver ore, which he stated that he had found in the hills on the

Bosnian frontier, where he assured me that any amount was to be obtained. His veracity I have no reason to doubt, although unable to proceed thither to confirm his statement by my own testimony. It is certain, however, that the mountains of Bosnia are unusually rich in mineral products. Gold, silver, mercury, lead, copper, iron, coal, black amber, and gypsum, are to be found in large quantities; silver being the most plentiful, whence the province has received the name of Bosnia Argentina. The manifold resources of the country in this respect have unfortunately been permitted to remain undeveloped under the Ottoman rule, while the laws laid down relative to mining matters are of such a nature as to cripple foreign enterprise. In this proceeding, the Turkish government has committed the error of adhering to the principles and counsels of France, which is essentially a non-mining country. In three places only has any endeavour been made to profit by the secret riches of the earth, viz. at Foinitza, Crescevo, and Stanmaidan, where iron works have been established by private speculation. The iron is of good quality, but the bad state of the roads, and the difficulty of procuring transport, render it a far less remunerative undertaking than would otherwise be the case. Good wrought iron sells at three-halfpence the pound. Were a company formed under the auspices of the British government, there is little doubt that they might be successfully worked, since there is nothing in the nature of the country to render the construction of a road to the coast either a difficult or expensive operation. Continuing our course on the right bank of the Narenta, we arrived at a lofty mound, evidently of artificial construction, situated at a bend of the river. Traces of recent digging were apparent, as though search had been made for money or curiosities. It was just one of those positions where castles were built of yore, its proximity to the river being no small consideration in those days of primitive defences. A short distance from its base were two tombstones, sculptured with more than ordinary care and ability. One of these represented a man with a long sword and shield, faced by a dog or fox, which was the only portion of the engraving at all effaced.

At a spot where a spring issued from the rocks, we were met by a party of Irregulars, shouting and firing their matchlocks in a very indecorous manner. They were doubtless going their rounds, bent on plunder, as is their wont; and living at free quarters. The place where we encountered them was wild in the extreme, and well adapted for deeds of violence. It was indeed only in the preceding spring, that a murder was committed on that very spot. Nor was it the first murder that had been done there. Some years previously two Dalmatian robbers concealed themselves behind the adjacent rocks, with the intention of murdering two Turks, who were carrying money to Bosna Serai. These Turks, however, detected the movements of the assassins, and as one of the Christians fired, one of the Turks returned the shot, each killing his man. Sequel: the second Christian ran away; the surviving Turk carried off his companion's money in addition to his own.

At one part of our route a landslip of large dimensions had taken place, covering the slope to the river with large stones and blocks of red marble. This, as well as white, black, and gray marble, are found in large quantities in the surrounding hills. The river at this point is turgid and rocky, and there are two or three rapids almost worthy of the name of falls. The narrow rocky ledge, which constitutes the only traversable road, immediately overhangs the water, having a sheer descent on the right of nearly 200 feet. The edge of this precipice is overgrown with grass and shrubs to such a degree as to render it very dangerous. Indeed it nearly proved fatal to my horse and myself: the bank suddenly gave way, and but for the fortunate intervention of a projecting ledge, which received the off fore and hind feet of the former, we should inevitably have been picked up in very small pieces, if anyone had taken the trouble to look for us.

Having now journeyed about ten hours from Mostar, our road wound to the left, leaving the Narenta at its confluence with the Drechnitza, which waters the valley of the same name. Close to its mouth, which is spanned by a neat two-arched bridge, a Ban is said to have lived in former days; and a solitary rock projecting from the hills on the left bank is pointed out as his favourite resort. The summit of this is smoothed off, and traces of an inscription still exist, but too much defaced to be deciphered.


CHAPTER XVI.

Wealthy Christians--German Encyclopædia--Feats of Skill--Legend of Petral--Chamois-hunting--Valley of Druga--Excavations--Country Carts--Plain of Duvno--Mahmoud Effendi--Old Tombs--Duvno--Fortress--Bosnian Frontier--Vidosa--Parish Priest--National Music--Livno--Franciscan Convent--Priestly Incivility--Illness--Quack Medicines--Hungarian Doctor--Military Ambulance--Bosna Serai--Osman Pacha--Popularity--Roads and Bridges--Mussulman Rising in Turkish Croatia--Energy of Osman Pacha.

The family with whom we purposed spending the succeeding days were reputed to be the wealthiest of the Christians in that part of the country. It will perhaps convey a more correct impression of their means, if we say that they were less poverty-stricken than others. A few cows, some half-dozen acres of arable land, and a fair stock of poultry, constituted their claim to being considered millionaires. The household consisted, besides father and mother, of two rather pretty girls, two sons, and their cousin, who cultivated the land and hunted chamois regularly every Sunday. Besides these there were some little boys, whose only occupation appeared to be to bring fire for the pipes of their elders. Our arrival, and the prospect of a bye day after the chamois, threw all the men of the party into a state of great excitement. Minute was the inspection of our guns, rifles, and revolvers, the latter receiving much encomium. An old Turk, who had been summoned to take part in the morrow's excursion, eyed one of those for some time, and at length delivered himself of the following sentiment: 'They say there is a devil: how can this be so, when men are so much more devilish?' I am afraid the salvation of Sir William Armstrong, Mr. Whitworth, &c. &c., would be uncertain were they to be judged on the same grounds. While waiting for our dinner of fowls made into soup and baked potatoes, the sons brought a book, which the priest, with more regard for preserving his reputation for learning than veracity, had told them was a bad book. It proved to be a German Encyclopædia. On hearing this one remarked, 'Oh, then it will do for cigarettes.' While regaling ourselves on wine and grapes, which one of the hospitable creatures had walked twelve miles to procure, we received visits from the male population of the village, who, like all the people of the valley, are much addicted to chamois-hunting. Their conversation, indeed, had reference exclusively to sport, varied by a few feats of skill, hardly coming under the former name. One villager asserted positively that he had seen a man at Livno shoot an egg off another's head. This was instantly capped by another, who affirmed that he had witnessed a similar feat at the same place. His story ran thus: 'At the convent of Livno, all the Roman Catholic girls of the district are married. On one occasion a young bride was receiving the congratulations of her friends, when a feather which had been fastened across her head became loosened, and waved around it. A bystander remarked that he would be a good shot who could carry away the feather without injuring the head. The girl upon hearing this looked round and said, "If you have the courage to fire, I will stand." Upon which the bystander drew a pistol and shot away the truant feather.'

The valley of Drechnitza is wild and rocky, but sufficiently wooded to present a pleasing aspect. The timber is in many places of large girth, and might easily be transported to the sea. It is invested also with more than common interest by the primitive character of its people, and the legends which associate it with the early history of the province.

At present only four villages remain in the valley; that where our hosts lived being the most ancient. They indeed spoke with pride of having occupied their present position since before the conquest, paying only a nominal tribute of one piastre and a half until within the last thirty years, since which time their privileges have been rescinded.

On the left bank of the Drechnitza, about half-way between its confluence with the Narenta and the house of our hosts, is a small valley named Petral; it derived its name from the following circumstances:--For seven years after the rest of Bosnia and the Herzegovina had been overrun by the Turks under Mehemet II., the people of this valley maintained an unequal combat with the invaders. The gallant little band were under the orders of one Peter, who lived in a castle on the summit of a height overlooking the plain; this plain could

only be approached by two passes, one of which was believed to be unknown to the Turks. In an evil hour an old woman betrayed the secret of this pass, and Peter had the mortification one morning of looking down from his castle upon the armed Turkish legion, who had effected an entrance during the night. Like a true patriot, he sank down overcome by the sight, and died in a fit of apoplexy; whence the valley has been called Petral to this day.

A few ruins mark the spot where the church stood of yore, and four tombstones are in tolerably good preservation. Beneath these repose the ashes of a bishop and three monks; the date on one of them is A.D. 1400.

Early the following morning we started for the bills, where the chamois were reported to be numerous. After about three hours' climbing over a mass of large stones and rocks, the ascent became much more precipitous, trees and sand taking the place of the rocks. In course of time we reached a plateau, with an almost perpendicular fall on the one side, and a horizontal ridge of rock protruding from the mountain side beneath. Four of the party, which numbered eight guns in all, having taken up positions on this ridge, the remainder, with a posse of boys, made a flank movement with the view of taking the chamois in reverse. The shouting and firing which soon commenced showed us that they were already driving them towards us from the opposite hills. The wood was here so thick that occasional glimpses only could be obtained of the chamois, as they came out into the open, throwing up their heads and sniffing the air as though to detect the danger which instinct told them was approaching. Two or three of the graceful little animals blundered off, hard hit, the old Turk being the only one of the party who succeeded in killing one outright. The bound which followed the death-wound caused it to fall down a precipice, at the bottom of which it was found with its neck dislocated, and both horns broken short off. If the ascent was difficult, the descent was three-fold more so. The rocks being the great obstacle to our progress, the mountaineers managed well enough, jumping from one to another with the agility of cats; but to those unaccustomed to the kind of work, repeated falls were inevitable. How I should have got down I really cannot say, had I not intrusted myself to providence and the strong arm of one of those sons of nature.

The strong exercise which I had taken rendering me anything but disposed for a repetition of the sport on the ensuing day, M.G. left me on his return journey to Mostar, while I proceeded on my solitary way. This, however, was not so cheerless as I had anticipated, as the two sons of the house expressed a wish to accompany me as far as Livno on the Bosnian frontier, where their uncle, a village priest, held a cure. For several hours we remained on the left bank of the Drechnitza, which we forded close to its source. On the heights upon our right, fame tells of the existence of a city, now no more; and it is certain that a golden idol weighing 23 lbs. was found in the locality. Buoyed up by hopes of similar success, fresh gold-diggers had been recently at work, but with what result I am unable to say.

Bearing away now to the W. we entered the valley of the Druga, a little rocky stream. Two roads were reported practicable, the longer taking a winding course past Rachitna, the other, which I selected, being more direct, but far more rocky and difficult; the ascent at one point was more severe than anything I ever recollect having seen.

Leaving Druga we descended into the plain of Swynyatcha, a small open space, which is again connected with Duvno by a pass. The hills on the left of this pass are called Liep, those on the right Cesarussa. Here, too, report speaks of the existence of a city in former days, and the discovery of a large hag of gold coins, like Venetian sequins, has induced some speculative spirit to commence excavations on a large scale. But these, I regret to say, have not as yet been attended with any success. A very fair road has been recently made through this pass, and the traffic which has resulted from it ought to convince the people of the utility of its construction. We met many ponies carrying merchandise from Livno to Mostar, while long strings of carts drawn by eight bullocks were employed in carrying wood to the villages in the plain of Duvno. These carts are roughly built enough, but answer the purpose for which they are intended, viz. slow traffic in the plains. The axle-trees and linch-pins are made of wood, and indeed no iron at all is used in their construction. The plain of

Duvno is one of the largest in the province: its extreme length is about fifteen miles, and villages are placed at the foot of the hills, round its entire circumference. The most important of these is the seat of a Mudir, to whom I proceeded at once on my arrival. Although afflicted with a hump-back, he was a person of most refined manners. His brother-in-law, Mahmoud Effendi, who is a member of the Medjlis, was with him, and added his endeavours to those of the Mudir to render my stay at Duvno agreeable. Having complimented the great man upon the appearance of his Mudirlik, he laughingly replied, 'Oh, yes, they must work because it is so cold'--a statement which I felt anything but disposed to question. The wind was blowing down the plain at the time in bitterly cold blasts, and I understand that such is always the case. The vegetation appeared good, in spite of a seeming scarcity of water.

The people of the district are nearly all Catholics, which may be attributed to its proximity to Dalmatia and the convents of Bosnia. They are orderly and well-behaved, according to the Mudir's account; but I also gathered from some Catholics to whom I spoke that this good behaviour results from fear more than love, as the few Turks have it all their own way. In the centre of the plain are some old tombs, some of a sarcophagus shape, others merely rough flat stones, whilst here and there interspersed may be seen some modern crosses--a strange admixture of the present and the past. After a somewhat uncomfortable night in the one khan which the town possesses, I presented myself with early dawn at the house of the Mudir. Although not yet 8 o'clock, I found him with the whole Medjlis in conclave around him. Thence the entire party accompanied me to inspect the fort, or such part of it as had escaped the ravages of time. It was rather amusing to see the abortive attempts at climbing of some of these fur-coated, smoke-dried old Mussulmans, who certainly did not all equal the Mudir in activity. The fort is a quadrilateral with bastions, and gates in each of the curtains; in two of the bastions are eight old guns, dismounted: these are all of Turkish manufacture, some having iron hoops round the muzzles.

In the SW. corner is a round tower, evidently copied from the Roman, if not of genuine Roman origin. For what purpose the fort was built, or by whom, I was unable to learn. It is said, however, to have been constructed about two centuries ago[U], and there is a Turkish inscription on it to that effect; but, as I have said before, no reliance can be placed upon these. There are many buildings within the walls, and one mosque is reputed to have existed a hundred years before the rest of the fort.

Shortly after leaving the village we arrived at the frontier line of Bosnia and Herzegovina, which is, however, unmarked. Already the country presented a greener and more habitable appearance, which increased as we continued our journey. Towards evening we stopped at a little village named Vidosa, where the uncle of my hunting companions held the post of parish priest. Having sent one of his nephews in advance to warn him of my arrival, he was waiting to receive me, and invited me to stay at his house with great cordiality. Notwithstanding that the greater portion of it had been destroyed by fire a few months previously, I was very comfortably housed, and fully appreciated a clean bed after the rough 'shakes down' to which I was accustomed. That the kitchen was luxuriously stocked, I am not prepared to say; but the priest was profuse in his apologies for the absence of meat, proffering as an excuse that Roman Catholics do not eat it on Friday, a reason which would scarcely hold good, as I arrived on a Saturday. Of eggs and vegetables, however, there was no lack. Vegetable diet and dog Latin are strong provocatives of thirst, and the number of times that I was compelled to say 'ad salutem' in the course of the evening was astonishing. The old priest appeared more accustomed to these copious libations than his younger assistant, who before he left the table showed unmistakable signs of being 'well on.' Both vicar and curate wore moustachios, and the flat-topped red fez, which distinguishes their profession. The curate had received a certain amount of education at one of the Bosnian convents, whence he had been sent to Rome, where he had, at any rate, attained a tolerable proficiency in Italian, and a few words of French. Another occupant of the house, who must not be allowed to go unmentioned, was the priest's mother, a charming old lady in her ninety-seventh year. Age had in no way impaired her faculties, and she was more active and bustling than many would be with half her weight of years.

In the evening the nephews made their appearance, having dined with the domestics. The remaining hours were devoted to singing, if such can be termed the monotonous drawl which constitutes the music of the country. In this one of the brothers was considered very proficient: the subjects of the songs are generally legendary feats of Christians against the conquering Turks, which, however little they may have conduced to bar the progress of the invaders, sound remarkably well in verse. Sometimes, as in the present case, the voice is accompanied by the guesla, a kind of violin with one or three strings.

The priest, although a man of small education and strong prejudices, appeared to be possessed of much good sense. He deplored the state of things in Herzegovina, and said that much misery would ensue from it, not only there, but in all the neighbouring provinces. As an instance of the severity of the government demands, he mentioned that 1,400 baggage-horses had been recently taken from the district of Livno alone, as well as more than 400 horse-loads of corn, for all of which promises of payment only had been made. For the accuracy of his statements I am not prepared to vouch, but I give them as they were given to me. He did not, however, complain so much of the quantity, as of the injudicious mode of proceeding, in making such large demands at one time.

A few hours took me to the town of Livno, on the outskirts of which is the Catholic convent. Mass was being performed at the time; but I found the Guardiano, 'Padre Lorenzo,' and one of the Fratri disengaged. After keeping me waiting for some time in a very cold vaulted room, these two came to me, though their reception of me contrasted very unfavourably with that of the simple village priest. The convent is for monks of the Franciscan order, of whom there were five besides the Superior. It is a large, rambling, and incomplete building of white stone, and in no way interesting, having only been completed about six years. After mass came dinner, which was provided more with regard to quantity than quality, and at which the holy men acquitted themselves á merveille. Excepting a young priest of delicate appearance and good education, the brethren appeared a surly and ill-conditioned set. So ill-disguised was the discontent conveyed in the ungracious 'sicuro' vouchsafed in reply to my petition for a bed, that I ordered my traps to be conveyed forthwith to the best khan in the town, and, having failed to find favour with the Christians, sought the aid of the Mussulman Kaimakan, from whom at any rate my English blood and Omer Pacha's Buruhltee insured me advice and assistance.

The Austrian Consul also received me with much civility, and most obligingly placed his house at my disposal, although compelled to start for Spolatro on business. For some reason best known to himself, he begged of me to return to Mostar, insisting on the impracticability of travelling in Bosnia in the present state of political feeling. This, coupled with the specimen of priestly civility which I had experienced in the convent of Goritza, inclined me to alter the route which I had proposed to myself by Foinitza to Bosna Serai. In lieu of this route, I resolved upon visiting Travnik, the former capital of Bosnia, before proceeding to Bosna Serai (or Serayevo, as it is called in the vernacular), the present capital of the province. In fulfillment of this plan, I started on the morning of the 21st, though suffering from fever and headache, which I attributed to a cold caught in the damp vaults of the Franciscan convent. With each successive day my illness became more serious, and it was with difficulty that I could sit my horse during the last day's journey before reaching Travnik. At one of the khans en route, I put myself into the hands of the Khanjee, who with his female helpmate prescribed the following remedies:-

-He directed me to place my feet in a basin of almost boiling tea, made out of some medicinal herbs peculiar to the country, the aroma from which was most objectionable. He then covered me with a waterproof sheet which I carried with me, and, when sufficiently cooked, lifted me into bed. Though slightly relieved by this treatment, the cure was anything but final; and on my arrival at Travnik I was far more dead than alive. There an Hungarian doctor, to whom I had letters of introduction, came to visit me, and prescribed a few simple remedies. One day I hazarded the remark that stimulants were what I most required; upon which the learned doctor observed, with proper gravity, that brandy would probably be the most efficacious remedy, as he had often heard that English soldiers lived entirely on exciting drinks. Ill as I was, I could scarcely refrain from laughing at the drollery of the idea.

After a few days' stay at Travnik my medical adviser began, I fancy, to despair of my case; and on the same principle as doctors elsewhere recommend Madeira to hopeless cases of consumption, he advised me to continue my journey to Bosna Serai. The difficulty was to reach that place. Here, however, the Kaimakan came to my help, and volunteered to let out on hire an hospital-cart belonging to the artillery. I accepted his offer, and after a few days' stay at Travnik set forward on my journey to Bosna Serai. The carriage was a species of Indian dâk ghari, with side doors, but without a box-seat; it was drawn by artillery horses, ridden by two drivers, while a sergeant and gunner did escort duty. Fortunately the vehicle had springs, which must have suffered considerably from the jolting which it underwent, although we only proceeded at a foot's pace.

After three days' journey we reached Bosna Serai, where I was most kindly received by Mr. Z., the acting British Consul, and by M.M., the French Consul, with whom I stayed during the three weeks that I was confined to my room by illness.

Bosna Serai, or Serayevo, is probably the most European of all the large towns of Turkey in Europe. It is not in the extent of the commerce which prevails, nor in the civilisation of its inhabitants, that this pre-eminence shows itself; but in the cleanly and regular appearance of its houses and streets, the condition of which last would do credit to many a Frankish town. This happy state of things is mainly attributable to the energy and liberality of the present governor of Bosnia, Osman Pacha, who, notwithstanding his advanced years, has evinced the greatest desire to promote the welfare of the people under his charge. In the nine months of his rule which had preceded my visit, he had constructed no less than ninety miles of road, repaired the five bridges which span the river within the limits of the town, and introduced other reforms which do him honour, and have procured for him the gratitude and goodwill of all classes of his people. The system which he has introduced for the construction of roads is at once effective and simple. By himself making a small portion of road near the capital, he succeeded in demonstrating to the country people the advantages which would result from the increased facility of traffic. By degrees this feeling spread itself over the province, and the villagers apply themselves, as soon as the crops are sown, to making new portions of road, which they are further bound to keep in repair. This is obviously the first and most indispensable step in the developement of the resources of the country. It would be well for the Sultan were he possessed of a few more employés as energetic, able, and honest as Osman Pacha.

I regretted that the rapidity of his movements prevented my taking leave of him and his intelligent secretary. But, a few nights before my departure, an express arrived bringing intelligence of a rising in Turkish Croatia, near Banialuka. The news arrived at 9 P.M., and the energetic Pacha was on the road to the scene of the disturbance by 6 A.M. the following morning. The émeute proved trifling; not being, as was at first reported, a Christian insurrection, but a mere ebullition of feeling on the part of the Mussulmans of that district, who are the most poverty-stricken of all the inhabitants of the province.

CHAPTER XVII.

Svornik--Banialuka--New Road--Sport--Hot Springs--Ekshesoo--Mineral Waters--Celebrated Springs--Goitre--The Bosna--Trout-fishing--Tzenitza--Zaptiehs--Maglai--Khans--Frozen Roads--Brod--The Save--Austrian Sentry--Steamer on the Save--Gradiska--Cenovatz--La lingua di tré Regni--Culpa River--Sissek--Croatian Hotel--Carlstadt Silk--Railway to Trieste--Moravian Iron--Concentration of Austrian Troops--Probable Policy--Water-Mills--Semlin--Belgrade.

The shortening days, and the snow, which might now be seen in patches on the mountain sides, warned us of approaching winter, and the necessity for making a start in order to ensure my reaching Constantinople before the Danube navigation should be closed. My illness and other circumstances had combined to detain me later than I had at first intended, and I was consequently compelled to abandon the idea of visiting either Svornik or Banialuka, two of the largest and most important towns in the province. The former of these places is interesting as being considered the key of Bosnia, in a military point of view; the latter, from the numerous remains, which speak eloquently of its former importance. The navigation of the Save, too, having become practicable since the heavy rains had set in, I resolved upon the simplest route of reaching Belgrade, viz., that by Brod.

In coming to this decision, I was influenced also by my desire to see the valley of the Bosna, in and above which the road lies for almost the whole distance. No site could have been more judiciously chosen, than that in which Serayevo is built. Surrounded by beautiful hills and meadows, which even in November bore traces of the luxuriant greenness which characterises the province, and watered by the limpid stream of the Migliaska, its appearance is most pleasing. As we rattled down the main street at a smart trot on the morning of the 16th November, in the carriage of Mr. H., the British Consul, it was difficult to believe oneself in a Turkish city. The houses, even though in most cases built of wood, are in good repair; and the trellis-work marking the feminine apartments, and behind which a pair of bright eyes may occasionally be seen, materially heightens the charms of imagination. The road for the first six miles was hard and good. It is a specimen of Osman Pacha's handiwork, and is raised considerably above the surrounding fields, the sides of the road being rivetted, as it were, with wattles. At the end of that distance, and very near the confluence of the Migliaska and the Bosna, I separated from my friends, who were bent on a day's shooting. From the number of shots which reached my ear as I pursued my solitary journey, I should imagine that they must have had a successful day. The love of sport is strongly developed in the people of these provinces, and nature has provided them with ample means of gratifying their inclination. Besides bears, wolves, boars, foxes, roebucks, chamois, hares, and ermines, all of which are plentiful in parts of the country, birds of all kinds abound; grey and red-legged partridges, blackcock, ducks of various kinds, quail, and snipe, are the most common; while flights of geese and cranes pass in the spring and autumn, but only descend in spring. Swans and pelicans are also birds of passage, and occasionally visit these unknown lands. The natives are clever in trapping these animals. This they do either by means of pitfalls or by large traps, made after the fashion of ordinary rat-traps.

Before continuing my journey, I visited the hot springs, which rise from the earth at a stone's throw from the main road. Baths were built over them by Omer Pacha, on the occasion of his last visit to Bosnia, for the benefit of the sick soldiers, and such others as chose to use them. Besides two or three larger baths, there are several intended for one person, each being provided with a kind of cell, as a dressing room. The waters are considered most efficacious in all cases of cutaneous diseases, and were at one time in great request for every kind of disorder, real and imaginary. From what I could gather from the 'Custos,' I should say that they are now but little frequented. Leaving the Migliaska, which is here spanned by a solid bridge of ten arches, we crossed the Bosna in about half an hour. Scattered along the river bank, or in some sheltered nook, protected by large trees alike from the heat and the eyes of curious observers, might be seen the harems of various pachas, and other grandees connected with the province. After four hours farther march, we arrived at Ekshesoo, where 1 located myself in the khan for the night. My first step was to send for a jug of the mineral water, for which the village is famous, and at one period of the year very fashionable. The water has a strong taste of iron, and when fresh drawn, effervesces on being mixed with sugar, wine, or other acids. It is in great repute with all classes, but the Jews are the most addicted to its use. No Hebrew in Serayevo would venture to allow a year to elapse without a visit to the springs; they generally remain there for two or three days, and during that time drink at stated hours gallon after gallon of the medicated fluid. The following night I arrived at Boosovatz, where I left the Travnik road, which I had been retracing up to that point. The water of the Bosna is here beautifully transparent; and at about an hour's distance is a spring, the water of which is considered the best in Bosnia. The Pacha has it brought in all the way to Serayevo, yet, notwithstanding this, I saw many persons in the village suffering from goitre, a by no means uncommon complaint in Bosnia. The cause for the prevalence of this affliction is difficult to understand, unless we attribute it to the use of the river water, which is at times much swollen by the melting snow.

10th November: rain fell in torrents, much to my disgust, as the scenery was very beautiful. The road, which is a portion of the old road constructed by Omer Pacha, skirts the banks of the river, which winds sometimes amongst steep wooded hills, at others in the smooth green plains. At one point we were obliged to ford it; the stream was rather deep and rapid, and I certainly experienced a sensation of relief when I saw my baggage pony fairly landed on the opposite bank, without further injury to his load than a slight immersion. The fishing of the Bosna is not so good as that of the Narento and some other rivers of Bosnia and Herzegovina. Let me not be accused of a partiality for travellers' tales, when I say that trout of 60 lbs. have been killed in the latter province. In external colour these are veritable trout, the flesh, however, having a yellowish appearance, something between the colour of trout and salmon; the smaller fish are of excellent quality and are very abundant. Three hours after leaving Boosovatz we reached Tzenitza, a small town where a little trade is carried on. While sitting in the public room of the khan, the post from Brod arrived en route to Bosna Serai. The man who carried it came in wet and mud-bespattered, and declared the road to be quite impassable; a bit of self-glorification which I took for what it was worth. Had I not been pressed for time I should have myself been inclined to give way to the importunities of all concerned, to postpone my journey to Vranduk until the following day; but seeing no prospect of any improvement in the weather, I deemed it prudent to push on.

Another difficulty, however, here presented itself. The Tchouch of Zaptiehs positively declined to give me a guide; and it was only by sending for the Mudir, and threatening to write a complaint to the Serdar Ekrem, that I succeeded in obtaining one. This escort duty is the principal work of the mounted Zaptiehs. Ten piastres a day, or twenty pence, is what is usually paid them by those who make use of their services. They, of course, pay for the keep of their own horses out of their regular official salary. The rain now gave place to snow, which fell in considerable quantities for two or three days. The cold was intense, and it was only by halting at every khan, generally about three hours apart, that it was possible to keep the blood in circulation. On the morning of the 20th the sun shone out bright and comparatively warm, although everything bore a most wintry aspect. Beautiful as the scenery must be when spring has clothed the trees with green, or when the early autumnal tints have succeeded the fierce heat of summer, the appearance of the country clad in its snowy garments might well compare with either of these. The hills, rugged in parts, and opening out at intervals into large open plains, trees and shrubs groaning with their milk-white burden, or sparkling like frosted silver in the moonlight, and above all the river, now yellow and swollen, rushing rapidly along, produced an effect characteristic and grand.

About ninety miles from Serayevo the river becomes much broader, and swollen as it was by the recent rain and snow, presented a very fine appearance.

On its right bank stands the town of Maglai, which is prettily situated in the side of a basin formed by the hills, a craggy eminence apparently dividing the town into two parts. Behind these, however, the houses meet, sloping down close to the river's edge. On the very summit of the central mound is an old fort mounting five guns, which command the river, but would otherwise be of little use. The only means of communication between either bank, is a ferry-boat of rude construction. After leaving this town there still remained four hours of my journey to be accomplished, before arriving at Schevaleekhan, where I intended passing the night. Unaccustomed as I was to anything like luxury, I was positively staggered at the total absence of even the commonest necessaries of life. At Maglai I had endeavoured without success to buy potatoes, fruit, and even meat; but here neither bread, eggs, nor chickens, which are nearly always procurable, were to be found. Having received the inevitable 'Nehmur' to every one of my demands, I could not help asking what the inhabitants themselves eat; and being told that they lived upon vegetables, asked for the same. Judge, then, of my astonishment when told that there were none. Fortunately my kind friends at Bosna Serai had not sent me away empty-handed, or assuredly I should have felt the pangs of hunger that day.

At all times a khan is a painful mockery of the word hotel, as it is often translated. Picture to yourself a room about eight feet square, with windows not made to open, a stove which fills one-third of the entire space, and a wooden divan occupying the other two-thirds; the whole peopled by innumerable specimens of the insect creation, and you have a very fair idea of an ordinary khan. If there be a moment when one is justified in the indulgence of a few epicurean ideas, it is when inhabiting one of these abodes of bliss.

About an hour from Schevaleekhan we crossed an arm of the Bosna by means of a ferry-boat; a little farther on the left bank stands a town of 300 houses, built very much after the same principle as Maglai. Like that place it has an eminence, around which the houses cluster. This is also surmounted by a fort with three guns, two small and one large. The Mudir told me with no little satisfaction that it was the last place taken by the Turks, when they conquered Bosnia. Profiting by my experience of the previous day, I took the precaution of buying a chicken, some bread, and a few more edibles, on my way through the town. Provisions were, however, both scarce and execrable in quality. Meat is indeed rarely to be obtained anywhere, as sheep are never killed, and bullocks only when superannuated and deemed unfit for further physical labour. Chickens are consequently almost the only animal food known. The method of killing them is peculiar. The children of the house are generally selected for this office. One secures a very scraggy fowl, while another arms himself with a hatchet of such formidable dimensions as to recall in the beholder all sorts of unpleasant reminiscences about Lady Jane Grey, Mauger, and other historic characters. The struggling bird is then beheaded, and stripped of his plumage almost before his pulses have ceased to beat. The first occasion on which I saw one of these executions, I could not help thinking of a certain cicerone at Rome, who, albeit that he spoke very good French and Italian, always broke out in English when he saw a picture of a martyrdom of any kind soever; 'That one very good man, cut his head off.' The man had but one idea of death, and the same may be said of these primitive people, who look upon decapitation as the easiest termination to a half-starved life.

Leaving Kotauski, where I passed the night of the 21st, at 7 A.M., I reached Brod at 8.30 in the evening. The distance is considerable, but might have been accomplished in a far shorter time, had not the country been one sheet of ice, which rendered progression both difficult and dangerous. Each person of whom I enquired the distance told me more than the one before, until I thought that a Bosnian 'saht' (hour) was a more inexplicable measure than a German 'stunde' or a Scottish 'mile and a bittoch.' At length, however, the lights of Brod proclaimed our approach to the Turkish town of that name. On the left bank of the Save stands Austrian Brod, which, like all the Slavonic towns near the river, is thoroughly Turkish in character. Late as it was, I hoped to cross the river the same night, and proceeded straight to the Mudir, who raised no objections, and procured men to ferry me across. But we had scarcely left the shore when we were challenged by the Austrian sentry on the other side. As the garrisons of all the towns on the frontier are composed of Grenzer regiments, or confinarii, whose native dialect is Illyric, a most animated discussion took place between the sentry on the one hand, and the whole of my suite, which had increased considerably since my arrival in the town. My servant Eugene, who had been educated for a priest, and could talk pretty well, tried every species of argument, but without success; the soldier evidently had the best of it, and clenched the question with the most unanswerable argument--that we were quite at liberty to cross if we liked; but that he should fire into us as soon as we came into good view. There was therefore no help for it, and unwillingly enough, I returned to a khan, and crossed over early the following morning. At his offices, close to the river, I found M.M., le Directeur de la Quarantine, and general manager of all the other departments. He accompanied me to the hotel, which, though not exactly first-rate, appeared luxurious after my three months of khans and tents. I was somewhat taken aback at finding that the steamer to Belgrade was not due for two days, and moreover that the fogs had been so dense that it had not yet passed up on its voyage to Sissek; whence it would return to Belgrade, calling at Brod, and other places en route.

It therefore appeared the better plan to go up in it to Sissek, than to await its return to Brod. By this means I was enabled to see many of the towns and villages on the Bosnian, Slavonian, and Croatian frontiers. Leaving my servant and horses at Brod, I went on board the steamer as soon as it arrived. The scene I there found was curious. In a small saloon, of which the windows were all shut, and the immense stove lighted, were about thirty persons, three or four of whom were females, the remainder merchants and Austrian officers. The atmosphere was so oppressive that I applied for a private cabin, a luxury which is paid for, in all German companies, over and above the regular fare. I was told that I might have one for eleven florins a night. To this I demurred, but was told that any reduction was impossible; it was the tariff. At length the inspector came on board; to him I appealed, and received the same answer. After a little conversation, he agreed to break through a rule. I might have it for seven florins. No! well, he would take the five which I had originally offered; and so I got my cabin. That it was the nicest little room possible, I must admit, with its two large windows, a maple table, a large mirror, and carpeted floor; and a very much pleasanter resting-place than the hot saloon. The night was rainy and dark, and we lay-to throughout the greater part of it, as is the invariable rule on the Save, and even on the Danube during the autumn months. At eight on the following morning we touched at Gradiska. There are two towns of the name, the old one standing close to the river, and embellished with a dilapidated castle; the new town being about an hour's distance inland.

About noon we reached Cenovatz, which, like the other towns and villages on the frontier, might be mistaken rather for a Turkish than a German town.

The Castle of Cenovatz is an irregular quadrilateral, with three round and one square tower at the angles. It is now occupied by priests. It is interesting from its connection with the military history of the country. There, on a tongue of land which projects into the river, waved the flag of France during the occupation of the Illyrian provinces by the old Napoleon, while on the main land on either side the sentinels of Austria and Turkey were posted in close juxtaposition. Hence it has received the name of "la lingua di tré regni."

At six o'clock the same evening we entered the River Culpa, at the mouth of which is the town of Sissek.

It has a thrifty and cleanly appearance, and possesses two very fair inns. The saloon of one of these appeared to be the rendezvous of the opulent townspeople. Music, chess, billiards, and tobacco-smoke, appeared to be the amusements most in vogue; the indulgence in the latter being of course universal. Here I took leave of my companions of the steamer, whose loss I much regretted, especially M. Burgstaller, a gentleman of much intelligence, who requested me to examine his silk, manufactured at Carlstadt, for the International Exhibition. On the ensuing morning, I crossed the Culpa, and inspected the works connected with the new railway to Trieste. It is intended to be in a state of completion by the end of the coming autumn. Several Englishmen are employed on the line, but I did not happen to come across any of them; every information was, however, given me by a Croatian gentleman, who has the superintendence of one-half of the line. Moravian iron is used in preference to English, although its value on delivery is said to be the greater of the two.

Sissek was in ancient days a place of no small importance. There, Attila put in to winter his fleet during one of his onslaughts on the decaying Roman empire. Traces of the ancient city are often dug up, and many curiosities have been found, which would delight the heart of the modern antiquarian. The return voyage to Brod was not remarkable for any strange incident, the passengers being almost entirely Austrian officers. The number of troops massed by that power on her Slavonian and Croatian frontier would infer that she entertains no friendly feelings to her Turkish neighbours. These amount to no less than 40,000 men, dispersed among the villages in the vicinity of Brod, and within a circumference of fourteen miles. At Brod itself no fewer than 4,000 baggage-horses were held in readiness to take the field at any moment. It requires no preternatural foresight to guess the destination of these troops. They are not intended, as some suppose, to hold in check the free-thinking Slavonic subjects of Austria! Nor is that province used as a penal settlement for the disaffected, as others would infer. The whole history of Austria points to the real object with which they have been accumulated, viz. to be in readiness to obtain a footing in Bosnia, in the event of any insurrection in that province of sufficient importance to justify such a measure. The utility of such a step would be questionable, as climate and exposure have more than once compelled the Austrians to relinquish the idea, even after they had obtained a substantial footing in the province. The motives which would induce them to make another attempt are palpable enough; for, besides the advantages derivable from the possession of so beautiful and rich a country, Austria sees with alarm the increase of revolutionary principles in a province in such close proximity to her own. And yet she has small reason for fear, since no single bond of union exists between the Slaves on either bank of the Save.

But even if this were not the case, surely her soundest policy would be to support and strengthen in every way the Turkish Government, since their interests are identical, viz. the preservation of order among the Slavish nations of the world.

After leaving Brod, the banks of the river become flat and uninteresting; that on the Bosnian side is to a certain extent covered with low brushwood. After passing the Drina, which forms the boundary between Bosnia and Servia, it becomes still less interesting; the only objects of attraction being the numerous mills with which the river is studded. On the morning of the 29th we moored off the wharf at Semlin, but just too late to enable me to cross over to Belgrade by the morning's steamer. During the day, which I was compelled to pass in the town, I received much attention from General Phillipovich, who commanded the garrison, to whom I tender my sincere thanks. In the evening I crossed over to Belgrade (the white city), the capital of the principality of Servia.

SERVIA:

ITS SOCIAL, POLITICAL, AND FINANCIAL CONDITION.

CHAPTER I.

The erroneous notions prevalent throughout Europe relative to the internal condition of Servia, are mainly traceable to two causes. The first of these is the wilful misrepresentation of facts by governments to their subjects, while the other, and a far more universal one, is the indifference inherent in flourishing countries for such as are less successful, or which have not been brought into prominence by contemporaneous events. We English are operated upon by the last of these influences. We are contented to accept the meagre accounts which have as yet reached us, and which give a very one-sided impression, as is but natural, the whole of the materials having been collected at Belgrade. I am not aware that anyone has during the past few years written upon the subject; and having been at some pains to obtain the means of forming a just estimate of the character and condition of the Servian people, I must fain confess to very different ideas concerning them to those which I had previously entertained, based upon the perusal of Ranke and Von Engel, or the lighter pages of Cyprien Robert and Paton.

The retrograde movement, but too apparent, gives cause for serious regret, not only to those who are politically interested in the well-being of the country, but to all who desire to see an advanced state of civilisation and a high moral standard amongst a people who pride themselves on the universality of Christianity within their limits.

The present population is about one million, and is said to be increasing at the rate of ten per cent., but so crudely compiled are the statistics, that doubts may be entertained of the accuracy of this statement. Of this million of souls, 200,000 at the lowest estimate are foreigners; the greater portion being Austrian subjects, and the children of those Servians who on three separate occasions migrated to the northern banks of the Danube. What has induced them to return to their ancestral shores, whether it be Austrian oppression, or an unlooked-for patriotism, it is hard to say; but whatever the motives, they have not proved of sufficient strength to awaken the dormant apathy inherited with their Slavish blood. Save those who have settled at Belgrade, and who drive a most lucrative and usurious trade, they have sunk back contentedly to a level with the rest of their compatriots.

The scanty population is only one of the many signs of the decadence of a country for whose future such high hopes were entertained, and whose name is even now blazoned forth as a watchword to the Christians of Turkey. In reality, a comparison with most Turkish provinces, and more especially with those in which the Mussulman element predominates, will tell very favourably for the latter. Roumelia, for example, with a smaller area, contains a larger population, produces more than double the revenue, while land is four times as valuable, the surest test of the prosperity of a country. This last is easily accounted for by the lamentable indolence of the masses, who are contented to live in the most abject poverty, neglecting even to take advantage of a naturally fertile soil. Yet must it not be supposed that indifference to its possession prompts this contempt for the cultivation of land. There is probably no province so much enclosed, and where the mania for litigation in connection therewith is so rife as Servia. An insurmountable obstacle is thus thrown in the way of foreign enterprise, by the narrow-mindedness of the people.

The same want of energy has had the most baneful effect upon commerce, the very existence of which is merely nominal. Even at Belgrade the common necessaries of life are daily imported from the Austrian banks of the Danube. No one is more alive to the deplorable state of affairs than the reigning Prince, whose long residence in the capitals of Europe has familiarised him with their bustling scenes of thriving activity. Well will it be for Servia and himself, if he shall turn the experience which he has acquired to some practical account. Any doubts which he may previously have entertained regarding the misery of the country, and the moral degradation of his subjects, were removed effectually by all that he witnessed in a recent expedition into the interior--miserable hovels, uncultivated fields, magnificent forests wantonly destroyed, were the sights which met him at every turn. At length some restrictions have been placed on the wilful abuse of the greatest source of wealth which the country possesses. Nor are they premature, for the reckless destruction of the forests, combined with a failure of the acorns during the past year, produced serious distress. Already has the export trade of pigs diminished by one-third of the average of former years. This is immediately owing to the necessity of feeding them on Indian corn, a process which proves too expensive for their poverty-stricken owners, and which in this respect places the pig and its proprietor upon an equality. The latter live almost entirely upon maize and sliegovich, a kind of rakee made out of plums, and extremely fiery.

The mode of treatment of their women, an infallible sign of civilisation or the reverse, was brought prominently to the Prince's notice by the following circumstance:--Having, in company with the Princess, visited the cottage of a thriving pig-owner, he observed the presence of three daughters of the house. These young ladies showed unmistakeable signs of approaching old-maidism, and the parental philosophy settled the question of their future pretty conclusively. 'Why,' said he, in reply to a question put by the Prince touching the solitary condition of the damsels, 'should I allow them to marry, when each of them is worth more than three fat pigs to me.' Manners must have changed very much for the worse since the days of Ami Boué, or it is difficult to conceive upon what he founds his assertion that labour is not imposed upon Servian women. Indeed it would be surprising were it not so, when they are subjected by the laws of the land to the indignity of the bastinado, from which even men, save soldiers, are exempted in Mahometan Turkey.

The absence of that blind subjection to a bigoted priesthood which distinguishes the other Christian populations, would seem to indicate a certain independence of spirit, but unhappily the accompanying symptoms are not so encouraging. With contempt for its ministers, has come disregard for the ordinances of the Church, the services of which are but scantily attended. Yet notwithstanding the irreligion which is spreading fast throughout the land, little tolerance is shown for adherents to other than the Greek Church. For example, Catholics are compelled to close their shops on the Greek feasts, of which there are not a few, under penalty of a fine. In the same liberal spirit the mob are permitted to break the windows of such houses as are not illuminated on these occasions.

An ignorant and narrow-minded man is generally also vain. The same law is equally applicable to nations. A fancied superiority over the Christians of the other Turkish provinces cannot escape the notice of the most casual observer. That Servia has acquired some fame for military exploits is true, and far be it from me to detract from the praise due to her efforts to achieve and maintain her independence. The successes of their fathers, however, over the small irregular Turkish levies to which they were opposed, do not warrant the present population in indulging in the vapid boastings too often heard, of their ability to drive the Turks to Constantinople, were they permitted so to do. In a word, they forget that they owe their present position, not to their own prowess, but to foreign intervention; without which the province would probably have shared the fate of Bosnia, Albania, Epirus, and the Pashaliks of Rutschuk and Widdin, all which were as independent as themselves, but were reconquered by the Turks, no European power having extended to them the safeguard of a guarantee.

# HERZEGOVINA

Whether the protection accorded to Servia has worked beneficially is for my readers to judge. The abstract question of the advantages thus conferred admits of debate, and for my own part I believe the present miserable state of the province to be mainly owing to the European guarantee. She was not sufficiently enlightened to profit by the advantages presented to her, and the honourable self-reliance which was the result of a successful resistance to the Turkish arms has given place to a feeling of indolent security. Nor is this the worst. A principal feature in a country under guarantee is the total want of responsibility in those vested with administrative power. Upon this the Servian rulers presume to a preeminent degree, and indulge in many acts of presumption which would be impossible were they not fully alive to the fact that the conflicting interests of the guaranteeing powers, added to their own insignificance (which perhaps they overlook), exempt them from any fear of chastisement.

The principle of supporting the independence of a province forming a component geographical part of an empire, must have but one result, that of weakening the mother state, without, as experience has shown, ameliorating the condition of the province. Independently, therefore, of the drain upon the Turkish finances, for the maintenance of troops from time to time on the Servian frontier, to counteract revolutionary propaganda, her influence throughout her Slavish provinces is much weakened. Although in a position as anomalous as it must be unpalatable, the Ottoman Government deserves credit for abstaining so entirely from any species of interference in the internal affairs of the country; for be it remembered that the province is still tributary to the Porte. The hattischeriff of 1834, by which, on the evacuation of the country, the Sultan retained the right of garrisoning the fortresses, has never been strictly adhered to, and may at some future period lead to complications. Belgrade is secure from any efforts which may be made against it, but the other forts are hardly worthy of the name, and were only used as a place of refuge in case of attack. The Servians now complain of the infringement of the hattischeriff, and M. Garaschanin has but lately returned from Constantinople, whither he was sent on a special mission in connection with this subject. He endeavoured to procure an order for the withdrawal of all Mussulmans from the villages which they now occupy in the vicinity of the forts. This demand would appear just in the letter of the law, but for the neglect on the part of the Servian Government of one of the conditions, which was, that before resigning their property, the Mussulmans should receive an equivalent in money. The payment of this has been evaded, and the Porte consequently declines to interfere in the matter; should the Sultan hereafter accede to the demand, it would be no great sacrifice, as he would still retain

Belgrade. Situated as that fortress is, at the confluence of the Danube and the Save, surrounded with strong and well-ordered fortifications, and commanding every quarter of the town, its occupation in the event of hostilities would at once determine the fate of the province.

The city may be fairly said to represent the sum of civilisation in the country. In addition to 2,000 Austrian subjects, the population is of a very polyglot character, who, however much they may have added to the importance, have deprived the town of its national appearance.

CHAPTER II.

Before alluding to the financial or military resources, it will be well to pass in brief review the events of the past few years, of which no chronicle exists. These, if devoid of any special interest, tend considerably to our enlightenment regarding the much vexed question of a south Slavonic kingdom, and at the same time of Russia's prospects of aggrandisement south of the Danube. The neutral attitude preserved by Servia during the war in 1854-55, must have been a grievous disappointment to the Emperor Nicholas. Had she risen consentaneously with the irruption of the Hellenic bands into Thessaly and Epirus, the revolt might have become general, and would have been fraught with consequences most perplexing to the Sultan's allies. This neutrality may be attributed to the position assumed by Austria throughout that struggle, combined with the independence of Russian influence manifested by the then reigning family of Servia. No sooner was peace declared, than Russia applied herself to the task of producing a state of feeling more favourable to herself in the Slavonic provinces. While adhering to her traditional policy of fomenting discord, and exciting petty disturbances with the view of disorganising and impeding the consolidation of Turkey, she redoubled her efforts to promote her own influence by alienating the Greek Christians from their spiritual allegiance to the Archimandrite, and transferring it to the Czar. Nor to attain this end did she scruple to resort to presents, bribes, and even more unworthy means. That her efforts have not met with more signal success than has as yet attended them, is due to the indifference displayed by the people on these subjects.

One measure which was deemed most important was the substitution in Servia of the Obrenovitch family for that of Kara George. This occurred in 1858; and during the lifetime of Milneh, Russian influence was ever in the ascendant. The familiar roughness of tone and manner assumed by that Prince towards his uncultivated people procured for him great weight; while his astute cunning, his hatred of Turkey, and his Russian bias, would have given a most valuable ally to that power, had she procured his restoration before her armies crossed the Pruth. Fortunately no opportunity presented itself for him to promote actively the cause of his imperial master; and the two years which he survived his return to power are marked only by occasional ill-judged and bloodthirsty emeutes, as prejudicial to his people as they were ineffectual in overthrowing Turkish supremacy.

The eastern policy of France, during the Italian war, was subjected to many powerful conflicting influences. The chances of creating a diversion in the rear of Austria, owing to the unsettled state of the Turkish provinces, was probably thought of. Why the idea was abandoned is not for us here to enquire; but it may be in part attributed to the display of force which Turkey for once put forth at the right moment. Be this as it may, no disturbance took place until the winter of 1859, when, upon the withdrawal of the Turkish troops, fresh rumours of an insurrectionary nature were heard. These are well known to have been encouraged and circulated by the Servian Government, which calculated upon foreign support, at any rate that of Russia. But Russia has no wish to precipitate a crisis. The disastrous results of Prince Gortschakoff's mission have, at any rate, taught her the impolicy of plucking at the fruit before it is ripe. Her own internal reorganisation, moreover, occupies her sufficiently, and renders any active interference for the moment impracticable. Even were it otherwise, were Russia able and willing to renew the struggle in behalf of her co-religionists, the report of Prince Dolgorouki as to the amount of assistance likely to be derived from them, would hardly tend to encourage her in her disinterested undertaking. This envoy arrived at Belgrade in the latter part of 1859, while Prince Gortschakoff's charges were issued shortly after his return, and were doubtless based upon his reports. (Yet it is more than probable that the primary object of his mission was to enquire into and to regulate the revolutionary movements, which at that moment had acquired a certain degree of importance.) The Bulgarian emissaries told him frankly that no rising could be looked for in those provinces, unless Russia took the initiative. They reminded him that in 1842, when Baron Lieven visited Belgrade, the Bulgarians were induced by the promises of Prince Michael Obrenovitch to rise en masse. These promises were never fulfilled, and the insurrection was put down with great barbarities by the neighbouring Albanian levies. This single fact is tolerably conclusive as to the unreality of a south Slavonic insurrection, of which so much has been said, and to promote which so much trouble has been taken. Even were the discontent tenfold as deep-rooted as it now is, the Turkish Government might rely on the Mussulman population and the Arnauts to suppress any rising of the Christians. The chief danger to Turkey lies in the truculent nature of those whom she would be compelled to let loose upon the insurgents, and who would commit excesses which might be made an excuse for foreign intervention. The attainment of this ignoble end has been and still is the policy pursued by more than one power. Prince Milosch played admirably into their hands, not foreseeing that in the general bouleversement which would be the result, the independence of Servia might be disregarded. The invasion of the Bosnian frontier by bands of Servian ruffians was a measure well calculated to arouse the fury of the Mussulmans; and if such has not been the case, it may be attributed to the rapid dispersion of the miscreants. Little credit, indeed, accrued to Servia in these hostile demonstrations, for while the bands were composed of the lowest characters, and could only be brought together by payment, they quickly retreated across the frontier at the first show of resistance. It is significant that these bands were in nearly all cases led by Montenegrins, a fact which indicates the decline of that spirit of military adventure to which the Haiduks of old (robbers) could at least lay some claim. Discreditable as these proceedings were, worse ensued.

On the 5th of August a murderous attack was made upon a party of Mussulmans in the close vicinity of Belgrade, upon which occasion eight were killed and seventeen wounded. No fire-arms were used, probably to avoid alarming the garrison. The absence on that night from the capital of both Prince Milosch and his son, furnishes just grounds for suspecting them of complicity in the affair, while the presence of Sleftcha (notoriously a creature of Russia), and Tenko, among the murderers, clearly shows where and with what views the crime was devised. On the same night, five Mussulmans who were sleeping in a vineyard at Kladova, on the Bulgarian frontier, were murdered by Servians, while an attack was made upon a third party. The prospects of a country whose princes connive at, and whose ministers commit murder, cannot be very brilliant. Whether other atrocities might have met with the sanction of Milosch it is impossible to say, for death cut him off in the latter part of September, 1860, full of years and crimes. Not the least of these was the death of Kara George, who was treacherously murdered at his instigation. But let us pass from so unattractive a retrospect to a consideration of the character and policy of the living prince who now holds the reins of government.

CHAPTER III.

The appointment of Prince Michael to the vacant throne of Servia was the first step towards the substitution of hereditary for elective succession. One of the first measures of the new prince was to induce the Skuptschina, or National Assembly, to legalise for the future that which had been an infraction of the law. The sixteen years which intervened between 1842, when Michael was ejected, and 1858, when Prince Milosch was reinstated, were passed by the former in the various capitals of Europe. The high Vienna notions which he imbibed during that period have deprived him of the sympathy and affection of his semi-civilised subjects, as much as the uncultivated mind of his father deprived him of their respect. Nor does the lack of sympathy appear to be one-sided. And, in truth, that mind must be possessed of no ordinary amount of philanthropy which can apply itself to the improvement of a people at once so ignorant and vain, and who evince withal so little desire for enlightenment.

At the time of his accession the Russian element, as has been shown, was strong in the Ministry. Sleftcha and the Metropolitan were her principal agents. It was to be expected, therefore, that he would adhere to the family principles, and sell himself body and soul to his great benefactor. But it frequently happens that persons who have risen to unexpected eminence turn upon those by whom they have been raised. This would appear to be somewhat the case with Prince Michael, who certainly does not show the same devotion to Russia as did his father. It may be that he has not noted in the foreign policy of that power the disinterestedness which she so loudly professes. If such be his views, who can controvert them? To the character of the man, combined with his peculiarly irresponsible condition (owing to the guarantee), may be ascribed his present line of conduct. Ambitious, obstinate, and devoted to intrigue, his character is no more that of a mere puppet than it is of one likely to attain to any great eminence. At first, it must be acknowledged that he played into the hands of Russia most unreservedly. No endeavours were spared to stir up discontent and rebellion in the surrounding provinces. Little credit is due to the sagacity of those by whom these machinations were contrived. For example, petitions were sent to all the foreign consulates purporting to come from the Christian subjects of Turkey on the frontiers of Bosnia and Bulgaria, and setting forth the miserable condition to which they had been reduced by Mussulman oppression. The sympathy which might have been felt for the sufferers was somewhat shaken by attendant circumstances, which threw doubts on the authenticity of the letters. It appears that these arrived from the two frontiers by the same post, while, on comparison, they were found to be almost identical in form and wording.

Great results were also anticipated from the Emigration movement, to which the early part of 1861 was devoted. Russia, while endeavouring to promote the emigration of Bulgarians to the Crimea, did not discourage the efforts of Servia to induce them to cross her frontier with the view of settling. Several thousands did so, and these came principally from the Pachaliks of Widdin and Nish. Amongst these were many criminals and outlaws, who were admitted by the Servians, in violation of their charter. Considerable excitement prevailed, and subscriptions were set on foot for their benefit, but the movement appears to have died a natural death, as nothing is now heard of it. The émigrés cannot have been too well satisfied with the position in which they found themselves, since the greater number soon returned whence they came, in spite of Mussulman oppression.

Since the failure of this scheme, the Prince has applied all his energies to the acquisition of independent power. He first endeavoured to effect it by means of a deputation to the Sublime Porte. Failing in this, he resorted to the internal means at his disposal, and has gained his point. The principal objects which he had in view, and which he has succeeded in carrying out, were the declaration of hereditary succession, and the abrogation of the Ustag or Constitution, by which his power was limited. The Senate, as the deliberative body may be termed, originally consisted of 17 members. They were in the first instance nominated by the then reigning prince, but could not be removed by him, while vacancies were filled up by election among themselves. The whole of these rules he has now set aside, and, albeit he has given a colouring of justice to his proceedings by restoring the original number of members, and some other customs which had fallen into abeyance, he has virtually stripped them of all power. With great astuteness he induced the Skuptschina to deprive the Senate of legislative functions, and immediately afterwards to relinquish them itself, thus placing absolute power in his hands. This grossly illegal action has met with some faint resistance, but the Prince will without doubt carry out his wishes. He has only to fear internal discontent, as he is entirely independent by virtue of the guarantee, not only of the European powers, but even of Turkey. It is true that this very policy cost him his throne in 1838, but with years he has gained prudence, and he is now pursuing it with far greater caution. The Servians, too, having sunk immeasurably in the social scale, are less likely to stand upon their rights, or to give him the same trouble as heretofore.

Up to the present time all these schemes have weighed but little in the scale against the one absorbing ambition of his life. In a word, Michael is a hot Panslavist. Of this he makes no secret, and he has probably shared hitherto, in common with all Servians, very exaggerated notions of the importance which Servia would assume were the dismemberment of Turkey to take place. Their self-conceived superiority over the other Christians of European Turkey, induces the Servians to regard the northern provinces in the same light as do the Greeks the southern. The ambition of Michael, however, is not satisfied with the prospect of dominion over the undeveloped countries south of the Danube. His conversation, character, and previous history all point to one conclusion--that he aspires to sway the destinies of the Slavish provinces of Austria, and maybe of Hungary itself. His marriage with an Hungarian lady of the name, and it is to be presumed of the stock of the great Hunyadi family, would appear to give some consistency to these dreams. The chief drawbacks to its fulfilment are the unreality of the agitation among the Slavish populations, the power of Turkey to crush any insurrection unaided from without, and the honour and interest of Great Britain, which are staked on the preservation of the Ottoman empire from foreign aggressions. Although he may indulge in such day dreams, it is impossible but that a man of Prince Michael's calibre must be alive to all the opposing elements which will defer the accomplishment of them to a remote period. Notwithstanding natural prejudices, which in his case, however, are not very strong, it is probable that he now sees the inutility, and understands how visionary are the ambitious projects which he once entertained touching Servia. Such, at least, is the opinion of those who have the best opportunities of forming a correct judgement in the matter. Whatever may be his own intellect, whatever his ability to conceive and execute, Servia is too degraded to carry him through. To be the nucleus of a large kingdom, certain elements are necessary, in which she is strikingly deficient. Among these may be placed tried and flourishing institutions, unity of sentiment and purpose amidst all classes, and a due appreciation of the advantages of education and commerce; while last, but perhaps the most important of all, is civil and religious liberty of the highest order. In all of these, I repeat, Servia is eminently wanting.

A very slight glimpse also at her financial and military resources will show how far she is fitted to take even a leading part in any emeute which circumstances may hereafter bring about. The total revenue of the country has up to this time amounted to 200,000l. sterling. This has been raised by a tax of $5 levied on about 40,000 males. Nearly the whole sum is expended in paying and equipping the army, and in the salary of officials. Dissatisfied with the small amount of revenue, the Prince undertook, during the past year, to reorganise the taxation. An impost upon property was projected in lieu of the capitation tax, but having, unfortunately, started without any very well-defined basis, the system broke down, actually producing a smaller revenue than was yielded by the original method. Equally abortive, as might have been anticipated, was the scheme for raising a militia of 50,000 men. Presupposing, for the sake of argument, a strong military spirit to be rife among the people, the financial condition of the country would render the idea untenable, since it is with difficulty that the 1,800 soldiers who constitute the regular army can be maintained. Granting even the willingness to serve, and the ability of the government to pay them, the population of the country would not, according to ordinary statistics, furnish so large a force. The greatest number that could be calculated on in the event of war would be about 40,000 men, and these only in a war in which the national sympathy might be deeply enlisted. How many of this number would remain in arms, would probably depend on the amount of plunder to be obtained, and the nature of the resistance which they might encounter.

The matériel of the existing force is about on an equality with that of most continental armies. A portion of the troops are armed with rifles, and the remainder with unbrowned muskets. One battery of artillery forms the aggregate of that arm of the service. There are 70 guns at the arsenal at Kragiewatz, but they are all old and unfit for field service. A French Colonel has lately been imported to fill the combined offices of War-Minister and Commander-in-Chief. This, and, indeed, the whole of the recent internal policy, leaves very little doubt of the source whence emanate these high-flown ideas. It cannot be better expressed than as a politique d'ostentation, which is, if we may compare small things with great, eminently French. The oscillation of French and Russian influence, and the amicable manner in which their delegates relinquish the field to each other alternately, implies the existence of a mutual understanding between them. Whether this accord extends to a wider sphere and more momentous questions, time alone will show. Meanwhile, the Prince continues to indulge in dreams of a Panslavish kingdom, and of the crumbs which may fall to his own share, while he neglects the true interests of his country, with which his own are so intimately blended. Let him apply himself to the developement of her internal resources, to the promotion of education and civilisation among the people, and, above all, let him root out that spirit of indolence which has taken such firm hold upon all classes. It is his policy to do all this, that Servia may be in a position to assume that leading place among the Slavonic races which she arrogates to herself, should unforeseen circumstances call upon her to do so. With her he must stand or fall; therefore, setting aside more patriotic motives, self-interest renders it imperative on him to apply himself zealously to her regeneration.

With regard to his foreign policy, he cannot do better than act up to the conviction which he has himself more than once expressed, that 'the interests of Servia are identical with those of Turkey.' For, should the disruption of the Ottoman empire take place--the probability of which is at any rate no greater than in the time of our grandfathers--it will not be effected by internal revolution, but by foreign intervention; and credulous must he be who can believe in the disinterestedness of those who would lend themselves to such a measure. Thus, in the partition which would ensue, Servia might find even her former independence overlooked.

Let me add, that if I have alluded in strong terms to the condition of the people, I have done it in all sincerity, regretting that Servia should thus cast away the sympathy which, were she bent on self-advancement, would pour in upon her from every side. If, again, I may appear presumptuous in dictating the duties which devolve upon her Prince, I am prompted to it by the supineness which he has as yet evinced in promoting the desire for civilisation. Let him delay no longer, for, should events so dispose themselves that Servia should be weighed in the balance, she will, unless an amendment takes place, be indeed found miserably wanting.

CONCLUSION.

In conclusion, I would venture to call attention to the fact that the preceding pages were written before events had assumed the aspect which they now wear. Actual hostilities had not then commenced against Montenegro; the Turkish Government had not then contracted the loan which has opened up new prospects for the finances of the country.

That Omer Pacha has not already brought the war to a close is to be regretted, but let those who criticise the slowness of his movements weigh well all the disadvantages against which he has to contend.

It would be useless to enumerate these again, as they are alluded to more than once in the course of this volume. Suffice it to say, then, that if Cettigné be taken and Montenegro occupied before the end of the present year, Omer Pacha will have placed another feather in his cap, and will have materially increased the debt of gratitude to which he is already entitled.

APPENDIX.

The following is an extract of a letter from the young Prince of Montenegro, addressed to the Consuls of the Great Powers. The sentiments which it expresses are creditable enough, and, did his acts corroborate his words, he would be well entitled to the sympathy which he demands.

Cettigné, le 30 juillet 1861.


Monsieur le Consul,

## HERZEGOVINA

A l'occasion de la récente et grave mésure prise par la Turquie envers le Montenégro, je crois devoir rompre le silence et faire connaître succinctement à MM. les Consuls des Grandes Puissances qu'elle a été tenue depuis un an par le Montenegro vis-à-vis de l'empire ottoman.

Depuis mon avènement j'ai employé tout mon pouvoir à maintenir la tranquillité. Sur les frontières je n'ai rien négligé pour éloigner tout motif de collision, pour calmer les animosités séculaires qui séparent les deux peuples, en un mot, pour donner à la Turquie les preuves les plus irréfragables de meilleur voisinage.

Dans une occasion toute récente je me suis rendu avec empressement au désir exprimé par les Grandes Puissances de me voir contribuer autant qu'il était dans mon pouvoir au soulagement des malheureux enfermés dans la forteresse de Niksich. J'ai été heureux de pouvoir en pareilles circonstances donner une preuve de déférence aux Grandes Puissances, et de pouvoir répondre, comme il convenait à un souverain et un peuple chrétien, à l'appel fait à ses sentiments d'humanité. Je ne me suis point arrêté devant la considération d'un intérêt personnel.

End./